Stories at Happy Hour

Remember to "feel the feels"

Wishing you all the best!

♥ 3·12-22

Stories at Happy Hour

The Black Book of Love, Desire and Scandalous Fun

A.M. Hoot

Published by Tablo

Dedication Page

Pat ~ Thanks for being the light in the darkness.

Star ~ You are my everything.

Chapter 1

Oscar's

Keira takes out a magazine she has been waiting to read but hasn't found the time in her busy life "of working from home", to get to it. Keira used to work as a nurse in the hospital, but as she got older her knees started acting up. She transferred from the hospital setting to the out-patient clinical setting, working in research, which eventually gave her the opportunity to work from home. Keira is wearing her favorite Green Bay Packers sweatshirt. She has reddish, auburn hair, she styles it in a cute pixie cut. She has the most beautiful, fair skin; looking at her you know she's Irish and it's no secret, she is proud of it.

She is a regular at Oscar's. Oscar's is a blue-collar bar, within the city but not directly downtown. It is far enough away from the hectic downtown scene, but not too far of a drive for Keira to get to on a regular basis. The owner, all the wait staff, and most of the patrons know her well. Keira loves everyone and everyone loves Keira. Keira's drink, a bloody mary, with a lime wedge, a pickle spear with two olives, and a beer chaser, is usually at the table before she sits down. Keira always sits at the same square table that has four roll-away chairs. It is the fourth table on the far right of the bar next to the wall and is conveniently close to the popcorn machine. Sometimes an additional table and chairs get added depending on what randoms might join in on the happy hour fun.

Keira looked forward to the monthly happy hours with the girls. She loved getting caught up on the office gossip, what was going on with her friend's lives, their families, their love lives, especially one in particular, Alex. Alex continuously had something going on, either a new love interest or even better, love drama.

Keira usually arrives at Oscar's 20 minutes before everyone else so she can get her favorite seat that faces the door. Keira's seat gave her the perfect view of everyone who walked through the door and conveniently enough, a perfect view of the good-looking, young bartenders, Jeff and Josh. They look like brothers but aren't. One thing is for sure, they are definitely young, and they are definitely good-looking. They are both easily 6 feet tall and then some. Josh is a little broader than Jeff, but Jeff has been working out over the past few years and his body has turned from a scrawny, skinny, tall kid, to a young, buff man, that looks quite delicious these days. Jeff has his head clean-shaven and Josh has a full head of hair, blondish brown curly locks. Keira likes to have her popcorn bowls, two, one for each side of the table, and her first bloody Mary half drank if not on her second bloody Mary by the time the rest of the girls show up.

Keira was able to read through one page of her Housekeeping Magazine before Jess and Sadie arrived. Keira loved that magazine. It gave her all kinds of tips on how to be a better organizer, it gave her fresh new cooking ideas, and tips on how to keep the kitty litter fresh and clean smelling longer. Keira is 50, actually 50 plus but she refuses to let anyone know her true age. Her friends never thought of her as old, and as the years went by, they never thought she looked any older, and Keira was just fine with that.

She was happy to look up and see Sadie and Jessica walking in. They were both wearing their navy-blue work scrubs, and they were both laughing about something. Jeff looked up from the bar and said, "Well hello ladies, it's great to see you again," with a wink and the cutest smile ever. The girls continued to giggle and said hi- and then they ran over to see Keira. Keira quickly put her magazine away in her oversized bag and got up from her roll-away chair to give the girls a huge hug. Keira's hugs were the best hugs. She hugged as if it has been years since she has seen the girls. But in all honesty, this is a monthly happy hour, and sometimes, depending on how great or bad things are going, they might meet up a little more often. Keira could not wait to hear why the girls were laughing. She felt like she basically had to beg them to fill her in on what they were so giggly about.

Jess looked up at Keira and said, "Well, it's a long story." Keira looked at Jess with a disgusted look and said, "Alex is not here yet, we have time, come on, come on, fill me in, what's so funny?" Jess sheepishly confesses and says, "Sadie and I decided to go see the male strippers that were in town this past weekend." Keira choked on her popcorn, and said "The Tramps, The Lady, and the Goddamn Tramps?" Jess nodded yes; her face was a little pink. Sadie had a huge grin but said nothing, it only confirmed that it was true, from Sadie's reaction Keira knew it was a fun night by all. Keira was a bit hurt that she was not included on this little adventure, if anyone needed to see nice young, buff men, showing off their six-packs, toned asses, and their wangy dangs, dancing around as if they actually enjoyed teasing middle-aged women (or men for that matter), it was definitely Keira.

Chapter 2

Keira

Keira was a hardcore Green Bay Packers and Queen fan. She was a divorced woman, been divorced for decades, never had kids, and the whole time the girls have known Keira, they never knew her to be interested in men or dating. She was married many years ago, to her college boyfriend, they were best friends. They did everything together, they enjoyed all the same things, and when they graduated from nursing school, they both landed jobs at the same hospital. They got married and decided they loved being together so much that they didn't need to ruin it by having kids. Keira loved him and thought she was living the dream. They went on many camping trips, music festivals, and traveled with friends all over the country. They were very adventurous.

One day Keira came home early from work and found her husband in bed with another man, yes, another man, obviously another thing they had in common. It was too bad he couldn't tell Keira that he liked guys too. The betrayal was devastating and from that point on Keira swore off any idea of trusting another man and vowed she would never date or give her heart away. Love was fake in her eyes, nothing but lies and deceit. It took Keira a while to tell the girls the whole truth about her ex-husband. She was so embarrassed that the marriage was a failure, but that he cheated on her with a man; that was just way too humiliating on multiple levels. She felt like she was a fool not to know what was going on behind her back, in her own bed, and who knows where else. The true story about her husband's betrayal was hard for her to say out loud and admit to her friends because if she said it out loud, it really happened. The night she decided to share how she busted in on her husband with a dude, was a night the girls spent a lot of time drinking, laughing, crying, and drinking. Keira shared that she had a lot of harsh words with God about the whole situation. But then she prayed, she prayed not to love or even hate her ex. She prayed to feel indifferent towards him. She said that was the only way she could get through it. The girls thought Keira was wise and they all admired her. That night, Keira was relieved and thankful to have such great friends but even more thankful for strong drinks and tasty-looking bartenders.

Sadie

Sadie is a nurse, married, and has two daughters that are in grade school. Keira, Jess, and Alex think Sadie has a weird relationship with her husband; they try not to say too much about it because Sadie gets defensive when they ask her if he is gay. And not because of Keira's ex-husband being gay but because Sadie says her husband is not interested in sex. At ALL. What guy is not interested in sex? Sadie has tried date nights, even kinky date nights, which Alex convinced Sadie would work, even role-playing but shockingly the dude is just not interested. He ignores Sadie, like she is invisible, even when she wears a slutty or elegant, lacey lingerie, or even when she tried wearing nothing but whipped cream on her nibblets and posed, spread eagle on the kitchen table. The girls were dumbfounded. Even if he was having an affair, what guy would turn that down? A gay guy?! But maybe even a gay guy would jump at the chance. Sadie is an attractive lady. She's 45, has long curly, light brown hair, and a nice-shaped body with curves in all the right places, a smile, and a laugh that makes everyone do a double-take. Maybe Sadie's husband's "Johnson" is the issue? Maybe he is having a tough time getting it up? But still, there are medicines and things one can do to help with that. Alex has tried to talk to Sadie about having them come to one of Alex's sex toy parties as a couple. Alex is certain that they can find the cure to whatever is ailing Sadie's boring sex life. Sadie is annoyed by it, but she will never leave him. He's a decent father and she says at least he is not abusive; the bills get paid and they get along like roommates. She knew it could be a lot worse. Sadie is usually up for anything and always looked forward to the happy hours when she could attend. She liked hearing about what Alex was up to and like Keira, lived vicariously through her.

Jessica

Jess is a single, 27-year-old, who is about 6'1. Alex calls her amazon woman, mostly because Alex is about 5'1, with heels on. Alex and Jess constantly say they would gladly live a day in the other's shoes just to know what it feels like to be so opposite. Jessica is this vivacious, gorgeous, tall woman, with the most voluptuous body that would put the Kardashian's to shame. She has shoulder-length blonde hair, sometimes it's a dark brunette, but today, she is a blonde.

She moved to town two years ago, from a small country town in Iowa. She wanted a fresh start. She loved her family, her parents were great, but the opportunity for work in the area was scarce and she was ready for something new. Jess has never had a boyfriend. She is secretly hoping to find the guy of her dreams. She liked country boys, but she also had a fascination with being a doctor's wife. She wanted to have a family someday, the typical dream of a dreamy husband, having two kids, a boy and a girl, a big house with a white picket fence, and a dog, all of it.

Jess landed a surgical technician job at the same hospital Sadie and Alex worked at. Eventually, the girls met and became close friends. Alex felt a little bad for Jess, she was new to town, didn't have any family or friends around. Alex was happy to take her under her wing, show her around and keep her included whenever there was anything exciting going on.

Chapter 3

Keira still trying to get the scoop out of the girls gets distracted by Alex walking in the door. Alex was wearing a tight-fitting black top that showed off her girls a bit, layered by a caramel-colored leather jacket. She had fitted jeans and super cute bootie boots that made her look taller than she really is. For a petite thing, she really did have a nice figure, but she worked hard at it. She worked out so she could eat and drink what she wants when she wants. Alex walked in with confidence and looked directly at the bartenders; Jeff and Josh to say hello, and then turned her attention directly to Keira. Alex loves her bartenders; she loves bartenders period. Alex always said nothing was better than getting greeted by a tall, delicious old or young man, offering to service you at the bar. She said it's the best kind of relationship. They are expecting to make your drinks and you are expecting to pay. It was a WIN, WIN! There should be no surprises, and having a nice man deliver those services, is a bonus. Lady bartenders are fine, but of course, Alex would rather flirt with a guy. You know the saying don't eat or shit in your pool, or sandbox, whichever one prefers to play in; Alex had the same rule, no dating the bartenders anywhere she likes to frequent because if the relationship goes sour, she cannot go back to that bar or at least not for a while. Even though Josh and Jeff are tasty-looking there is no way she is going to jeopardize the comfort zone of Oscar's. It is no secret that Jeff and Josh fantasize about being in one of Alex's sex stories, but it will never happen.

Alex has been waiting all week to see Keira. Even though all four ladies do happy hour once a month, sometimes Keira and Alex get together just the two of them. Alex can't wait to be with Keira and fill her in on everything she is doing, or who she is doing. Even though there is a huge age gap; Alex and Keira have a lot in common, they have both been devastatingly hurt by a man and refuse to ever feel that sort of pain ever again.

Alex

Alex, short for Alexandra is 33-years-old. She is a petite blonde. Her hair flows to the middle of her back; she's pretty with defined features. She has amazing blueberry eyes that pop. Alex says they are "brilliant" whenever she gets compliments on them, and laughs and says, "That's what it says on the box anyway." Naturally, her eyes are brown, Bambi brown; don't shoot me, Bambi brown eyes, to be exact. No one knows why she covers them up with blue-colored contacts but regardless, the brilliant blues are mesmerizing on her.

Chapter 4

Alex was married to Darius McMasters, a motocross racer that stole her heart the day she laid eyes on him. She met him at a Halloween party that Alex's brother dragged her out to. Alex was cute and fun. Her brother couldn't understand why the heck she was still single. Alex was in her late 20's at the time and just never met the guy that tripped her trigger.

Alex told her brother, Brax, short for Braxton, that she would go to the Halloween party but only for an hour. The Halloween party was way out in the sticks somewhere in a small dinky town. There were about 50 people in a shed all dressed up and drinking. Alex was dressed up as a pregnant nun, while Brax and his wife went as vampires. Yes, Brax was married so no wonder he thought Alex was dragging her feet to find Mr. Right. Brax and his wife Desirae were high school sweethearts, who got married as soon as they could. They couldn't wait to be together and start a family. Brax and Alex came from a very religious background so if Brax wanted to start a family he needed to put a ring on it.

Brax knew a lot of the people at the party, he was so charismatic. People seem to gravitate to him. He knew something about everything and could keep the interest of just about anyone. He had a very high IQ and if he didn't know what a person was talking about, he would ask just enough questions to get enough information to partake in the conversation, and he would be funny and woo the crowd. He was always a blast to be around. While he was busy being the center of attention, Alex was on the search for a stiff drink. In her head, she kept thinking *Man, I want a captain diet. I hope they have captain here. I bet all they have is keg beer. I have a shit ton of captain at home. If I was at home I wouldn't be in this stupid costume, I would be in fuzzy pj's, watching a scary movie, and on my 4th captain by now.* Alex walked up to the designated bar area. A guy was bent over behind the bar getting solo cups. His head popped up, Alex and his eyes locked. He was wearing Yamaha blue racing gear, dressed up like a motocross racer. He had short dark hair, but the tips were bleached blonde. He was about 5'10, and hot as fuck. She had never laid eyes on such a beautiful man in her whole life. He smiled, and dropped the solo cups he just picked up, and said, "Hey! You want a drink?" All Alex could muster up for a response was, "Yeah, ok." As she visualized herself wipe the drool from her lips, she was thinking, *I'll take whatever you are willing to give, sweet baby Jesus.....my brother is a genius.* The hot man poured her a beer in a red solo cup and handed it over. Their eyes were locked. He had this amazing grin that flashed over his face as if he knew she was awestruck by his beauty. Yes, his beauty. He was Goddamn Beautiful, and she wanted to scream it. He had these crystal blue eyes that sparkled and matched his award-winning smile. He said his name was Darius, but Alex couldn't catch what he said, maybe she was so dumbfounded by his good looks, but she just looked at him as if to ask him what he said but didn't say anything. He stepped away from behind the bar area and closer to Alex. He smiled and laughed a genuine laugh and said, "I'm Darius. What's your name, are you from around here? I know pretty much everyone, but I haven't seen you around." Alex snapped out of her dumb gaze and said she was a pregnant nun. Darius laughed and said, "Oh are we staying in character? I'm sorry, I am a motocross racer." Alex laughed and said, "My name is Alex, short for Alexandra." She didn't like the name Alexandra because it was too formal. She knew Alex was kind of a butch name, but she didn't care, she's obviously a girl, and if anyone questioned her sexuality or anything that was their problem. Darius repeated her name, and said, "Wow! Alex! I was expecting Mother Teresa or Mary" he laughed, "but I like Alex." He smiled and looked so intently in her eyes. Darius said in a cute, flirty way, "So you like role-playing do ya?" Alex was just amazed by the specimen in front of her. He was PERFECT. He was tall but not too tall, he was built. Darius works out, Darius definitely works out. Alex could only think one thing...*what is underneath that Yamaha gear?* And without hesitation, her instinct was to grab his ass. She was so shocked that she actually grabbed his ass. Man, was it firm, good lord was it FIRM! She didn't know him, didn't know him from Adam, and didn't know anything about him if he was married or had a girlfriend, and if he did, was she at the party? What the hell was she thinking? He had a surprising look on his face and laughed and then he squeezed her ass. He said, "Oooo...you like playing a little grab-ass too. I think we are going to get along just fine."

Alex and Darius did hit it off, for about 10 minutes, and then his cell phone rang. He ignored it, and then it rang again, and again. Alex didn't know if it was a girlfriend or a buddy calling. Or maybe he was a drug dealer, and someone needed some "candy" for Halloween. He looked at his phone and apologized to Alex. He looked at Alex like he didn't want to answer the phone; he didn't want to stop talking to her but obviously, it must have been urgent, the person kept calling him. He answered the phone and got real quiet, he hung up quickly. He looked at Alex and said, "I gotta go – but I need your number. We are not done yet." Alex was disappointed but didn't want to come across that way, and said: "Oh your girlfriend calling and wanting you back home?" Darius looked at Alex and said he didn't have a girlfriend; worse he had a mother and he wasn't supposed to be out at the party. Alex sharply responded, "Well, how old are you? Holy crap!" He laughed and said he was 24, but he had to go, he would explain later, could he just have her number? Alex being the tough bird she liked to pretend she was, playing hard to get and all, rattled off her digits. He said, "Wait, say it again, I need to put it in my phone." Alex rattled it off again, and Darius repeated it and started putting it in his phone. He turned to walk away, and then came back to Alex for one more ass squeeze, smiled, and ran out of the shed. Alex kept thinking *he better have gotten my fucking number right. Ugh...he probably didn't. He was too pretty to listen and type at the same time. HA!* She laughed to herself. She was hoping she would hear from him, but she was betting she wouldn't.

When she returned home that night from the party, she had a message on her phone. It was Darius. He left three numbers for her to reach him. He wanted to see her again as soon as he could, and the feeling was mutual. They decided to meet at the Outback Steak House at 7:00 on Tuesday night. Alex was so nervous about the date. She knew he was hot, way too hot for her. The night of the Halloween party was the first and only time they had seen each other. He was dressed up as himself, while Alex was dressed up as a pregnant nun. The only thing he could see of her was her face, not her hair, not her body, her face, her big ass eyes, and her big ass nose. UGH!!! Why was he even interested in her? She decided to dress casually but cute. She didn't want it to appear like she was trying too hard. She went with her "go-to" pair of jeans. They were light-colored denim boot-cut jeans. They hugged her in all the right places, showed off her cute little ass, and her lean legs. She always felt good in those jeans. She wore a black Taking Back Sunday t-shirt and a short black leather jacket. She also wore black, chunky heeled booties to give her some height. She showed up at Outback at 6:55, not too early but not late. She hated it when people showed up late, it was a sign of them being inconsiderate and rude. She walked in and walked straight up to the bar. She figured if he wasn't there yet she could order herself a drink, calm her nerves, chill up at the bar and wait for him to show up, but as she was walking up to the bar she saw him at the corner of her eye sitting in a booth. She looked directly at him and their eyes locked. He smiled. She felt her face flush. He was wearing light-colored blue jeans and a button-down plaid shirt, un-tucked. Holy shit he was so fucking hot! She was nervous and needed that drink. He stood up right away and said, "Sorry, I got here early, I didn't know if they were going to be busy and I wanted to make sure we got a booth seat by the bar." He smiled and went on to say, "I guess I am a little nervous. I ordered a Captain. Can I get you a drink? What would you like?" Alex smiled with relief, holy crap he was here early, admitted he was nervous and was drinking a captain. She was starting to feel better already. "I'll have what you're having," she said. He looked at her and smiled, "A Captain Diet with a lime on the side it is then." Alex thought could this guy get any dreamier, what's the catch?

They sat opposite of each other. Alex was relieved to get a drink in hand and start sipping. Darius smiled at Alex and said, "So you're a blonde? I was wondering what color of hair you had." He smiled and Alex started laughing and went on to say she realized that he probably had no idea what he was agreeing to when they decided to meet up for dinner. For all he knew she could have been a pregnant skinhead. He laughed and said, "A smoking hot pregnant skinhead." Alex flushed again. He thought she was hot, not just hot but smoking hot. YES! She laughed.

They started talking about anything and everything. They talked about the party a bit. Apparently, it was his cousin's party. Alex didn't know who his cousin was and admitted that her brother dragged her out to the Halloween party. They talked a bit about Braxton. Alex ended up sharing with Darius that she and her brother were super close. They grew up in a really strict, religious home and they only had each other to turn to. She admitted she was devastated when her brother left home to go off to college. Brax asked his friends who were still in town, to keep an eye on his kid sister. Alex was invited to a lot of college parties and was able to get booze easily. She admitted that she drank a lot after her brother moved away. She was about 15 when Braxton left. Braxton was the only one who could truly relate to her.

Alex said that she was more of a daddy's girl when it came to her parents. Her dad worked as a heating and cooling guy, on his spare time he loved to tinker out in the garage, working on cars or building things. Alex found herself hanging out with her dad a lot if she wasn't hanging out with her brother. She would help her dad with doing little things like holding a flashlight or handing him tools. He usually had the radio on, and they listened to Elvis and Johnny Cash. As Alex grew older, she realized why her dad spent so much time in the garage. Her mom was a little hard to be around. She remembered as a child she would watch her dad grab her mom's ass and her mom snapped at him. When someone snaps at you every time you touch them, you eventually stop. After a while, he stopped touching her at all. There didn't seem to be any love or affection between her parents. Her parents fought a lot and her dad would retreat to the garage. At least he could find peace there. Her mom was constantly going off to church; there was

Monday night fellowship with the church ladies, Wednesday night bible study, and Friday night was choir practice for Sunday's church service, and it seemed like she was at church all day on Sunday. A lot of the conversation in the house was about church and what the pastor was preaching about. There was no conversation about what anyone else was doing or anyone else's interests.

Alex laughed and said when she thinks of her mom, she thinks of Carrie's mom. Carrie, from the movie, *Carrie*. Darius laughed, Alex said no she was serious. She identified with Carrie on multiple levels. Her mom was a nut. Her name was Sharon and Alex referred to her as Psycho Sharon. Alex said Sharon was off her rocker. Alex told him a story of when she was a little kid, maybe 6, she loved unicorns. She had unicorns hanging from her ceiling, and stuffed animal unicorns, unicorn everything. One weekend her parents went to some church revival thing and when they came back home, her mom went into Alex's room and ripped the horns off of every unicorn she owned, saying that they were of the devil, because they were magical creatures. Alex cried. She had no idea what she did wrong or what was wrong with the unicorns. Just the day before the unicorns were fine and her mom was ok with it, but one or two nights at some church revival thing and her mom comes back acting like a monster. Braxton, being around 10-years-old at the time, ran into his sister's room and yelled at his mom. He thought it was cruel and he didn't know why she was doing such a crazy thing. He hugged Alex and told her it would be ok, the unicorns were just horses now, the same thing just missing the horns. Alex didn't want plain horses. She liked the unicorns because they were magical and made the horses special and pretty. Braxton told her he would fix them. Braxton did too. He tried to put the horns back on the stuffed animals, he sewed the horns on the best he could. Alex laughed. Braxton was a good brother.

Alex said her mom was bat shit crazy and depending on which preacher she was following that month; her mom would switch her beliefs. Alex was surprised her mom never ended up in a cult-like the Jim Jones cult, where Jones coerced a mass suicide/murder of over 900 cult members, 300 of them being children. Murder by Kool-Aid. Yep,

Alex thought for sure that's how Sharon would get her, murder by food or drink.

Alex said her family had a rule that no matter what, they ate dinner as a family. The whole family had to be there, and it was required that everyone ate all the food on their plate. She laughed and said, "Thank goodness she only made liver and onions just a few times a year". There was one night where everyone in the family got extremely sick after dinner, but Sharon was not as sick as everyone else, Alex and Brax thought for sure Sharon was poisoning them. Sharon would talk about the pastor preaching about the evil in the world, and how they needed to protect themselves from evil. Brax and Alex could see Sharon offing the family to "protect" them from evil. Her mom was so warped. Alex hoped the craziness didn't run in the family. Darius chuckled. Alex assured him she had worse stories, but she didn't need to bitch about her mom all night. She loved her parents. They were her parents. It was just tough being their kid sometimes. She knew her dad loved her, but her mom, that love came with conditions and it hurt.

Alex asked Darius if he had any horror stories about his parents to turn the focus off of her and her tortured childhood. Darius said that he actually had a great relationship with his folks. They were chill. Not religious or anything, and very supportive of him, which was cool because the lifestyle he chose with wanting to go into motocross was not exactly a sure thing. It was a dream of his to go pro, and his parents supported it. Of course, he had a real job working with his dad and he enjoyed that too, but he wanted to make it big in Motocross. It was nice hearing him say so many positive things about his parents. Alex could tell he was being sincere and when he talked about his parent's he was joyful.

Alex heard one of her all-time favorite songs come on. She couldn't believe it. It was *Possum Kingdom* by The Toadies. She hadn't heard that song in ages. She started dancing in her seat a little. Darius said, "You like the Toadies?" She was shocked! He knew who they were? Alex nodded her head and said the Toadies were one of her favorite bands and the song playing was her favorite song. He agreed and called it a classic. He told her she should get up and dance. If she feels it, she should FEEL it. He said, "Take in all the feels." She laughed at him. There was no way she was going to get up and dance at Outback. There was no dance floor and there were people there trying to enjoy their dinner, they didn't want to see her dancing around. She told Darius it was kind of a dark song; people don't usually dance to it. He told her that she was dancing to it in her seat; she needed to get up on her feet. Darius could see that Alex was not going to move. She stopped dancing in her seat. He stood up and offered his hand. She grabbed it like she was in a trance. She instantly stood up without thinking, and they started dancing right by their table. The other customers looked up at them, and the bartenders glanced at them. Alex was nervous, but Darius was solely focused on Alex. Suddenly the music got louder, and Alex just kept looking at Darius, he was crazy, but he was fun and exciting. Alex and Darius sang and danced to the song as if they were out on a dance floor. Alex was mesmerized looking at Darius, he was hot, he could dance, and he didn't care what other people were thinking of them. Alex found that so refreshing. She felt like her whole life was a lie.

Alex's parent's church preached about God and God's love and forgiveness, but she didn't see a lot of that. From her experience, people from the church ended up being the worst people ever. They hid behind religion to control people. They did not show love or forgiveness, they judged and shamed people. She felt like she had to pretend to be something she was not to please everyone else. Whenever she thought about the church or religion, she always got in the mood to listen to Nine Inch Nails, *Terrible Lie* came to mind at the moment. She usually drank to numb all the feelings of hurt, pain, judgments, and rejection.

She wasn't numbing the feelings tonight though. She was feeling all the feels and she liked it. She liked being with Darius, she felt safe, confident, and free. Their song ended and as Alex and Darius went back to their booth, the bartenders and some of the patrons clapped. Alex's face turned red. This time instead of sitting opposite Darius she sat right next to him in the booth. She just wanted to be near him. She felt like there was this force pulling her closer to him. She had no control. When she sat next to him, he smiled at her and rubbed her leg gently. She touched his hand and they smiled at each other. From that moment on, they did not stop touching. They could not keep their hands off each other. Darius told her that he thought she was a great dancer and that she should dance whenever she feels it move her. He thought she danced like an angel like she was making love to the music, it consumed her and that turned him on. He told her whenever the music moves her to go with it. Don't worry about what other people are thinking and stop trying to please other people. You cannot please everyone all the time, the only person you have control of is yourself, so please yourself. If you feel like dancing, dance. Alex blushed. She always thought she was a crazy dancer, but maybe he liked a little crazy.

They ate dinner and had a few more drinks. They talked as if they had been friends forever, friends that couldn't keep their hands off each other that is. The night was ending, the restaurant was closing, and it was time for them to say goodbye. Darius holding Alex's hand walked her out to her car. He told her he had a really good night, maybe one of the best nights he has ever had. Alex felt the same but didn't want to admit it. She just smiled and nodded her head in agreement. He leaned in and moved a piece of hair that was stuck to her bottom lip and then he kissed her. It was gentle, sweet. She kissed him back and then she kissed him more deeply and then kissed him again and again. Finally, she let go of him. He smiled a big smile and said, "Correction, this HAS been the best night of my life." She laughed at him. She was embarrassed and laughed a little more, "Yeah, I really like the steak here" she said with a wink and got in her car. Darius said he would call her later. He told her to drive home carefully because he wanted to see her again.

She started driving home and screamed out loud to herself. That was the best date she had been on and the best night of her life. She felt like she was in a movie. He was so cool, so dreamy, she couldn't get enough.

Chapter 5

Six months later Alex and Darius were still dating. It was a Friday night and Darius and Alex just got home to Alex's place. They were dancing at the Starlite bar all night. Alex was famished. She told Darius she would put a pizza in the oven, he nodded his head. Alex started the oven, picked a pizza out, and saw a bag of plain potato chips sitting out. She ripped open the bag and put a huge handful of chips in her mouth. She turned around to offer some to Darius and as she turned around, she saw him down on one knee, with a jewelry box open. There was a 3 stone, princess cut diamond ring in the box. It was gorgeous. Her mouth still full of potato chips, Darius says, "I bought this ring three months after I met you. I thought the three stones were fitting. It stands for the past, present, and future. I can't remember my life before you, and I don't want to. All I know is what we have here and now, and I want it forever." Alex still had a mouthful of chips; her eyes were bulging out and she wasn't moving. Darius started to sweat a little, he was happy he didn't purpose to her right when he bought the ring, if she is freaking out now, he would have totally scared her away three months ago. He nervously laughed and continued talking, "I know it's only been six months, but there is never going to be another love like ours, so why not?" Alex's eyes welled up in tears. The tears rolled down her cheeks. All she could think was holy shit, he wants to lock us in. He wants to marry ME??? She was all in from the first time she laid eyes on him. There was no question in her mind. She started nodding her head, yes, trying to quick chew the chips in her mouth and swallow, so she could scream yes, YES! YES! hysterically. He nodded at her to confirm, "Yes?" She was laughing and crying at the same time and screamed "Yes... yes, I'll marry you." He stood up and picked her up, and swung her around the kitchen. He hollered "Yes!" and said she just made him the happiest man. She was still crying. She was in shock, but deliriously happy.

They got married six months later. They were married before they even knew each other for a full year. Their relationship was ignited and fueled by passion. Darius made Alex feel alive and Alex excited Darius. Darius was protective and supportive of Alex, he loved her unconditionally and she knew it. She never felt a love like that and knew they were lucky to have what they had. Darius taught Alex to feel all the "feels" in life. Not to walk through life numb. He didn't want her to have any regrets. He wanted her to pursue her passions, talk freely, dress freely, find herself, be herself, and feel herself. She loved that he truly cared so much about her, he was so nurturing. Alex loved Darius so much it scared her. She almost felt like she wasn't a whole person until she met him. He made her whole, and ALIVE.

Chapter 6

Alex said the sex with Darius was amazing, out of this world amazing, but their make-up sex was almost an out-of-body experience. To have that much passion for someone, felt dangerous. Alex freaked out when she thought Darius was taking too many risks. Him needing to feel all the feels and all while he was riding his bike. She did not want him to get hurt. She was so worried he might get in an accident. He took too many risks, he challenged himself to go faster, try different tricks and jumps, and Alex was scared. She kept reminding him that it wasn't just him anymore it was the two of them now and she could not live without him. He was pissed at her that she didn't have enough faith in him that he could do it. It wasn't that she didn't have faith that he could do it, she knew he could do it. It was all the other idiots on the race track she didn't have faith in. She knew he could do whatever he put his mind to, she just didn't know if he would always survive and come back home to her after it was all done. Most of the guys on the track were reckless and huge thrill-seekers. They didn't care if what they were doing could hurt themselves or someone else. Darius understood she was scared but she had nothing to be afraid of, he would always come back home to her, he promised. Unfortunately, that was the one promise Darius did not keep.

Shortly after Darius and Alex's two-year anniversary, Darius was driving on his way home from work on a blizzard-like winter night. His truck slid on black ice. The truck flipped, and rolled over multiple times, crossing lanes, and landing in a farm field. Darius being the risk-taker he was, was not wearing his seat belt, he went straight through the windshield and died instantly upon the crash.

Alex was devastated. She felt as if she died that night, except her body was still wandering the earth. She was angry he was gone and the agony and the heartbreak she felt was indescribable. No matter how hard she tried to blame God or try to convince herself that there must not be a

God, she was reminded that there had to be a God. He created Darius. Only a god could create someone so perfect, and so perfect for her. Even though she only had three years with him, at least she had three years with him. When he purposed to her, he said there was no other love like theirs'. She was pretty certain there were millions of people who will never know that kind of love, so for that, she was thankful that she knew that love, she felt that love, and as Darius would say, she felt all the feels.

Chapter 7

Keira couldn't wait to rat out Jess and Sadie to Alex. Those bitches went to watch Lady and The Tramps and didn't think about taking her. What the hell? Before Keira could say a word, Alex walked up to the table and gave Keira, aka...Sex Kitten,(Alex's nickname for Keira), a huge, long hug. Keira needed the hug and so did Alex. Their connection was undeniable. Alex and Keira were the first to start the monthly happy hours. They shared so many heart-to-heart stories with each other over many drinks, they talked about love, heartbreak, family, and God, all in that order, and after a drunken night, they decided their life-long mission was to start a brothel. Keira would be the Madame, and Alex would be in charge of getting the clientele and hire appropriate help to service the customers. After that drunken night, Keira's new name was Sex Kitten, it was so fitting. Keira appreciated the sexy name. It made her feel special, and she was so elated that someone like Alex would befriend someone like her. Keira was one of Alex's best friends, she confided in her with everything, and never felt judge, or afraid of a horrible reaction from Keira. She felt safe with her and would never give up the relationship she had with Keira for anything.

Somehow word got out that Alex and Keira met for happy hours on the regular, so people inquired about the happy hours and started showing up. Keira and Alex designated monthly happy hours for any riffraff that wanted to come, but then there would be secret happy hours for just Keira and Alex where Keira could get all the juicy details of Alex's rendezvous and adventures. She loved living vicariously through Alex, and Alex loved being able to share her stories with Keira, knowing it was in confidence and she would never judge, Alex, spared no details.

Alex ordered a bloody, no salt around the rim, not spicy, and a beer chaser. That was always her first drink at Oscar's. She looked at the table and saw Keira's beer chasers sitting there, she must be on drink five now, according to the full beer chasers. Keira did not care for beer chasers, she ordered them for Alex, and she only ate half of her pickles and olives, those were for Alex too.

Keira forgot all about the Tramps and was hoping that Alex had something juicy to share with the girls. Keira was dying for some excitement. Keira was known to be Alex's little black book. She kept track of all the guys Alex met, dated, and screwed. She knew all their nicknames and their "unit's" nicknames too. Keira was always amazed by how Alex would pick up some of these guys, some of them bartenders, she did have a thing for bartenders, but a lot of them were not. Alex dated her fair share of doctors, lawyers, regular businessmen, guys with blue-collar jobs, one guy was even going to school to be a priest. Keira still had no idea how Alex swung that. Keira looked at her friend in awe. She thought the world of Alex and just wanted her to be happy.

Chapter 8

Keira was happy Alex was getting out, but she had no idea how she had the energy to work full time, go to school full time, be out all hours of the night, and survive off of little to no sleep. Keira knew Alex didn't like being at home. Home was not home when there was no Darius there. Alex shared some things with Keira a few times which made Keira worry for Alex. She didn't think she should go home alone some nights. Keira even offered to have Alex stay with her for a while, but Alex laughed it off and sarcastically said, "No, I need to feel the feels Keira, only way I can get through it." She made it a point to say get through it, not over it. She would never get over Darius, ever! And if any of her so-called concerned friends tried to hint that she should get over him, move on, or whatever their "friendly" line was, Alex was quick to tell them to fuck off. She was feeling her feels.

Keira remembered vividly the time when she and Alex met for drinks one Monday night. It was well over a year ago. Alex messaged Keira out of the blue on a Monday morning and asked if she could meet her at Oscar's after work around 4:00ish. Keira said absolutely, she couldn't wait and since this was unplanned, it must have been really juicy. 3:45 rolled around and Keira was sitting at Oscar's waiting for Alex to arrive. She had her bloody sitting in front of her with the beer chaser and all the fixins' that came with it, her bowl of popcorn, just one since it was just her and Alex, and she waited. Alex showed up at 3:50. She walked in the door wearing her navy-blue work scrubs and looked a bit wiped out. Keira thought oh no, either it was a really good night, or it was a really bad night. Did she sleep at all? Alex looked up and said hi to the bartender, Josh. Josh smiled, winked, and said, "Hello darlin'." She looked over to find Keira at her usual table and instantly she felt a sense of calmness and peace fall over her. She felt safe just looking at her sweet, dear, trusting friend, who loved her unconditionally. She quickly walked, almost in a skipping fashion, up to Keira and hugged her tight and long, Keira didn't even get a chance to get out of her chair. Keira laughed and said, "Hi Sweetie. You smell so good like always, is it that Armani stuff?" Alex nodded yes, she had two "go to" perfumes, Aqua Di Gioia by Armani or Cool Water by Davidoff.

Josh brought over Alex's bloody just the way she liked it, no salt on the rim, not spicy, extra garnishes, and a beer chaser. What a good boy, Alex thought. That's what she liked about that place. They knew her well and they always gave her what she wanted, without her having to ask for it. A great quality she looks for in every man, she giggled to herself.

Alex took a sip of her bloody, ate an olive, and slammed her beer chaser. She looked at Keira and said, "I hope I don't disappoint you today. I don't have anything juicy to tell you. I just needed to see you. We can talk about whatever you want I just can't go home yet." Keira was concerned and cocked her head to one side and asked Alex if something happened last night? Alex looked at her and shook her head, she didn't know exactly how to tell her friend what happened. Alex took another drink and said, "How are you?" Keira gave her a wiseass smirk and said she was doing fine. She was doing so fine she could have stayed at home with Bump, Whisper, and Tobey, her three cats, if she knew Alex was going to invite her to come out for drinks and just stare at her.

All jokes aside, Keira was concerned about Alex and wanted her to spill, spill whatever it was she needed to get off her mind and chest, just get it out. Alex laughed and said, "Oh you want me to feel the feels?" She rolled her eyes. Keira looked at her and said, "I want you to tell me about your night. Do we need to order shots? What's up?" She was trying to lighten the mood when she mentioned shots. Alex laughed and said, "No, we should wait to do shots for the next time Jesus comes to happy hour." Jesus was one of Alex's friends, just a friend. His real name was Tim, but they called him Jesus because Alex thought he looked like a Jesus. He was a huge pot smoker. He was high all the time and Keira and Alex loved him for it. He would always calm the mood down. He would have great one-liners like, 'Don't lie, it will make baby Jesus cry' or 'Don't worry about the hill, just chill'. He had long, shoulder-length, brown hair. He usually dressed in jeans, sporting a band t-shirt, usually the Doors or the Grateful Dead, and a flannel. He had a sweet face and he laughed all the time. Whenever he came out for happy hour, he demanded shots, usually Patron tequila. Keira and Alex had a rule when taking shots, if they started drinking shots, they had to leave the bar within 15 minutes, otherwise, if they waited any longer than that, the shots would kick in and they wouldn't be able to drive.

Since Keira wasn't going to let it die, Alex shared with her what happened the night before. Alex said she had a rough day. Something triggered her, she didn't say what it was, maybe she didn't know what it was, if she did, she didn't say. Alex just said she had a rough day. She went out to meet a few friends at a local bar. There was a local band playing so she thought why not.

Alex wasn't feeling the music or the company, so she decided to just go home. Her plan was to pour a glass of wine, take a bath, listen to soft music and crash early. Her body and mind needed the rest. Alex walked into her home and shouted at Google, "Hey Google, play 3 AM In My Feelings." A song by The Weekend came on. She walked into the bathroom and started her bathwater. She liked her bathwater hot, so hot it would burn the average person. She went into her bedroom, looked at her bed, it was big, empty, and uninviting. She started taking off her clothes. She was down to her panties and realized she needed to get a bottle of wine out. She walked into the kitchen; she grabbed a smooth and sweet California red blend and poured almost half the bottle in her wine glass. She walked back into the bathroom, lit some scented candles, poured some bubble bath in the bathtub, turned off the bathroom light, took off her panties, and slowly sat down into the bathtub. She yelled, "Hey Google, play Stateless music." And then quickly after, she yelled, "Hey Google, turn up the volume". An hour or so passed, Alex woke up to the song *Bloodstream* by Stateless. Alex sunk lower into the bathtub and started crying. She whispered to herself, feel the feels as if she could hear Darius whispering those words in her ear. She sat up, and she lifted her glass of wine to the ceiling as if she was toasting to someone. "Hey D! Here I am feeling ALL the feels. And guess what? It fucking sucks. I miss you. I miss your face. I miss your laugh. I miss you so fucking bad. I hate being here without you. It hurts! My fucking heart has been ripped from my chest. It's gone. You're gone and you promised me." She cried some more. At that moment she contemplated doing something she would never want to admit to anyone, but she really did not want to live in a world that didn't have Darius in it.

At that moment, Alex imagined Darius was with her, straddled behind her in the tub like he did so many times. She imagined him holding her, touching her, washing her hair, washing her back, caressing and kissing her. She must have been really buzzed because she could almost feel him, it felt so real. How she wished it was real. She fantasized that he was singing along with the song while he was playing with her hair and kissing the back of her neck. She cried and kept hearing him say, feel all the feels.

Alex finished her glass of wine, eventually got out of the bathtub, dried off her wet soapy body. She massaged her body with oil and got dressed for bed. It was late. She was drained, and she needed to be up for work in 4 hours. She slept hard and fast. Morning came way too soon. She woke up and messaged Keira asking if they could meet for drinks.

While Alex shared the story, she cried, she was shaking. Keira could see the pain all over Alex's face and it was heart-wrenching. She couldn't say or do anything to help her sweet friend. All she could do was be there, and she was always there. That's when Keira wondered if Alex should stay with her for a while. Keira knew Alex needed to feel the feels but if at any time the feelings got too intense, she wanted Alex to know she could always stay with her, anytime, with no questions.

Keira and Alex looked at each other in silence for a few seconds, and then a tearful Alex wiped her eyes, smiled, and said, "I know Jesus isn't here, but I think we better have some shots." Keira smiled back, "Shots it is." Both ladies raised their hands at the bartenders, Josh and Jeff. Jeff arrived at the table and asked if they needed more drinks. Alex ordered two rounds of Patron and the tab. When the shots arrived. Keira picked up her shot glass and cheersed to Alex, "To feeling all the feels." Alex nodded her head, smiled and they both downed their shots. Alex picked up her second shot glass and cheersed it to Keira and said, "To good friends who are the light in the darkness." Keira smiled with tears in her eyes and they both slammed their shots and got up from the table.

Chapter 9

When Keira started having knee problems, she asked for a transfer from the hospital to the clinic setting. They found her a research job, located on the floor where Alex worked, working with one of Alex's doctors. Keira started on the floor while Alex was away on personal time off. Keira heard all about the young girl that worked on the floor who recently lost her husband tragically in a car accident. It was awful. People were talking about it all over, at the desk, in the halls, and in the lunchroom. Everyone was whispering about Alex and how sad it was that she was a widow already at such a young age. Keira didn't know who they were talking about, but her stomach ached for the stranger.

A week past and Alex came back to work. It was hard for her. She was sad and she knew her co-workers were sad for her. She walked into the clinic and felt like people were looking at her. She heard whispers while she walked down the halls, some people just stared, and some walked up to her crying and offering hugs. When it was lunchtime, Alex opted against going to the lunchroom. It would have been horrible, full of awkward silence, people staring at her, or worse yet, people asking her how she was or saying they were sorry. Alex knew they all meant well but Alex just couldn't be around it, around them. She wanted to do her job, go home, hide in her bed, and stay away from anyone who knew her, or knew her and Darius and their life together.

Alex grabbed a yogurt. She didn't have much of an appetite these days. She walked down the hallway to find an open examining room to crash for 20 minutes or so during her lunch break. The last door on the right, at the end of the hall, was shut. The lights on the outside were shut off, indicating the room was empty. Alex pushed open the door. There was a woman that Alex had never seen before sitting at the desk typing away. She thought maybe she was a resident and just found a random room to do some work, but the lady looked older than the typical resident, maybe she was a visiting doctor? The lady looked over at Alex and smiled cheerfully and said, "Hello. Do you need the room?" Alex sheepishly laughed and said she was actually looking for a place to crash and then apologized for interrupting. The lady smiled and said, "Well, there's a couch in here and you are welcome to it. I am happy to dim the lights. The desk light is all I need. My work is mostly reading so I won't make any noise and I'm leaving for lunch in 10 minutes, so then you'll have the room to yourself."

Strangely, Alex felt comfortable with this lady even though she had no clue who she was. Alex smiled, shrugged her shoulders, and said, "OK." The lady introduced herself and said her name was Keira. She was new to the floor, working on a two-year research project for one of the doctors. Alex then nodded her head; that made sense now. Alex started walking towards the couch and told her that her name was Alex. Alex explained that she worked up at the desk, then she laid down on the couch and dozed off.

Keira's heart sank as she looked at the young girl. She was so petite, she looked like she weighed maybe 90 pounds soaking wet. Her scrubs were a little baggy. Keira heard about Alex's husband's death and understood the want or need to be alone. Keira turned off her computer and turned the lights completely off and left the room.

Keira came back to her office about 30 minutes later and Alex was gone. She looked at the couch where Alex took a nap and smiled. Two hours had passed, and Keira heard a knock on the door. She looked up, and Alex peeked her head in. Alex smiled and said, "Hey, I just wanted to say thanks for letting me crash on your couch. I am sure that was weird having someone sleep on your couch while you are trying to work." Keira smiled and told Alex not to worry, the couch was not hers, it was just in her office space, so if Alex ever needed it, she was free to use it any time, whether Keira was in the office or not. Alex smiled and told Keira she might regret she ever said that.

The next day, it was getting close to lunchtime and Alex decided to go down to Keira's office. Alex knocked on the door and there was no answer. She cracked the door open a bit, and the room was empty. She was a little disappointed. She kind of wanted to see Keira's friendly face. She was cheerful, but not over the top cheerful. Alex turned off the light and positioned herself on the couch.

Twenty minutes later the door opened. The light from the hallway woke Alex up. It was Keira. Keira walked into the room and saw that Alex was there. She kept the office light off and put her desk light on. She started up her computer and began to work. Alex could smell french-fries. It smelt delicious. She loved French fries. She couldn't remember the last time she had a French fry. She hasn't eaten much lately, nothing sounded good, nothing tasted good, and some days she would just plain forget to eat. Just then her stomach started making noises. She was a little embarrassed. She sat up. When she sat up, she saw a white styrofoam container sitting at the edge of Keira's desk. Alex instantly knew where the yummy smells were coming from. Keira looked at her and said, "Oh hi, I hope I didn't wake you." Alex looked at her and said "No, not at all, it's all good. I need to get back to work anyway." Keira could see Alex looking at the to-go box and she laughed, "Are you hungry, I actually brought that for you. I only eat half my lunch," Keira looked down at herself, laughed some more, and said she should only eat half her lunch, "So I was thinking you might want the other half? I didn't touch any of it. I asked the wait staff to split the order in half when I ordered. I went with the classic cheeseburger and fries, you hungry?" Alex smiled and said yeah actually she was. She told Keira she hadn't had fries in forever, so she was going to dominate Keira's leftovers. Alex opened up the container and chowed down. She was not shy about it. It tasted sooo good. It smelt soooo good. Keira smiled as she worked. She was happy to see Alex eating. At least she knew she would get one meal in that a day.

Chapter 10

Alex ended up visiting with Keira more and more. They started sharing lunch and took turns paying for the meal. They became close friends. Almost a year had passed, and Alex asked Keira if she wanted to go out for a drink. She was in the mood to get out but didn't want to hang out with anyone but Keira. Keira thought a drink would be nice. They went to Oscar's. It was near Keira's house and it was her favorite place to go.

Keira was at Oscar's when Alex arrived. Keira was seated at a table. She had a bowl of popcorn on the table and she was sipping on a bloody mary. Alex walked in and looked around. She saw the bartenders, nodded her head as to say hi, and kept searching the crowd until she saw Keira. Keira looked up, smiled, and mouthed "Hi," as she waved. Alex smiled back and walked quickly to the table. "Hey, sorry if you have been waiting for a long time, the last patient took forever. How are you? What's up with the sweatshirt, you know you live in Minnesota, right?" She laughed. Keira was sporting her Green Bay Packers sweatshirt. Keira rolled her eyes and laughed. The bartender came by and asked Alex what she wanted. Alex looked at Keira's bloody and it looked pretty good, it was almost gone. Keira chimed in and said the bloody marys there were very tasty. Alex ordered a bloody mary but she didn't want it spicy, no salt on the rim and she wanted extra fixins' with a beer chaser. After she was done with the order, she looked up at the bartender and flashed him a huge grin, and said, "Thank You, Baby!" She was so excited to be out and to be out with Keira.

They stayed out until the bar closed and talked about everything under the sun. Keira had one bloody mary after another, but she ordered them exactly the way Alex liked them. She gave Alex most of the garnishes and all the beer chasers. Alex drank the beer chasers and had multiple captain diets. She was feeling good. Keira shared with Alex about her husband cheating on her with a man. Alex swore never to say anything to anyone about it, she knew even though it happened 20 plus years ago, it was still painful, and people like to talk. Alex opened up about Darius. It felt good getting it all out. She liked talking to someone who didn't know who he was and didn't know Alex and Darius as a couple. It gave her the opportunity to share their story.

Alex even shared with Keira that she always had problems falling asleep and staying asleep even as a little kid. She told Keira about this farmhouse she and her family lived in for six months. Her parents were covering a pastoral leave at a church in a small rural town in northern, Minnesota that consisted of maybe 4,000 people. The farmhouse was owned by an elderly couple, Elmer and Betty Bailey, who owned 500 acres. The elderly couple built the farmhouse when they were young, and only had 2 acres of land, over time they acquired more land. They never had any kids of their own. When they were in their 30's they took in foster kids for about 30 years. Alex heard that the Bailey's would have the foster kids help them with chores on the land such as; picking corn and manning the fields, but most of the time the kids enjoyed playing on the farm. There was a huge treehouse that Mr. Bailey helped the kids build. Over time, foster kids would come and go, but none of them stuck around. Alex thought it was weird that none of the kids, not even one, stayed to work on the farm. The Bailey's were so kind to give them a place to stay and care for them, but no one stayed. Alex understood that it was a boring town, but still, didn't anyone care for this couple, who gave so freely of themselves?

When the couple turned 65 years old, they built their dream house nearby the old farmhouse. Since they weren't fostering kids anymore, they must have gotten lonely because they turned their dream house into a bed and breakfast, calling it Bailey's Bed and Breakfast, and started renting out the old farmhouse. The church put Alex's family up in the farmhouse while her parents were covering the pastoral leave.

Alex was 10 and her brother Braxton was 14 years old when they lived in the farmhouse. When they were kids their family moved around a lot, with every move Brax and Alex would take turns having the first choice of their room. Since Braxton got the first choice at their last house, Alex got the first choice in the farmhouse. It was a two-story farmhouse with five rooms and one bathroom. Two bedrooms on the main floor. And three small bedrooms upstairs. Alex said she wanted a bedroom upstairs. Brax took the room next to the family room on the main floor and their parents had the master bedroom on the main floor. Alex got all three bedrooms upstairs. She made one room her bedroom. Another room her schoolroom for when she needed to do homework and the last room was the nursery for her babies.

When they first moved there Alex and Brax liked living on the farm. It was summer-time and they got to run and play all day long. They were allowed to roam on the property and the Bailey's even told the kids they could pick corn and eat it fresh off the cobb, as much as they wanted, it was sweet corn and the best corn Alex and Brax ever had. The Bailey's noticed how much Alex and Brax liked spending time picking and shucking corn, that they ended up paying them to pick and shuck corn for them, and all the sweet corn collected went to the farmer's market.

When Alex and Brax weren't picking corn, they played hide and seek in the fields or played in the treehouse that Mr. Bailey made with the foster kids. The treehouse was huge. Brax thought about 10 kids could hang out in the treehouse comfortably. Alex and Brax wished they could take sleeping bags out to the treehouse and stay overnight but their parents would not allow it. It would have been really cold at night, considering even though it was summer, overnight temps could get down to the '40s.

Mr. Bailey told Brax and Alex they could work on the treehouse to make it their own seeing as it had not been used in over a decade. Brax spent a lot of time working on the treehouse switching out bad boards with new boards. Once school started Brax met some boys that would come over and help him out on the treehouse. Alex had a hard time meeting friends at school. She was quiet and kept to herself. She only wanted to play with Braxton and his friends.

Alex thought of herself as a tomboy. She wanted to be one of the boys. When she was at home she would run around the house without a shirt on like her brother and her family would always say that one day she wouldn't be able to do that anymore. Well, that day came. One night, Brax wanted one of his friends to sleep over and he told Alex that she needed to keep her shirt on. Alex didn't understand why and Brax told her, "Because you are a girl, and now that you are getting older, you are turning into a big girl, getting big girl parts like mom." Alex didn't know what he meant. She didn't like the tone in his voice. She was hurt. He said, "You are starting to get boobs, and you need to wear a shirt and mom should get you a bra. I don't want my friends looking at you, looking at your boobs!" Alex cried all night. She was devastated. She thought her brother was mad at her for getting boobs. She didn't want boobs. She wished she could be like Braxty. She didn't hang out with Braxton or his friends for a while. She thought Braxton didn't want her around now because she had boobs. She was a bit embarrassed that they found out about her boobs. While Alex told Keira the story, she laughed. Alex continued to tell Keira that she wandered off and hung out by herself a lot. She discovered that the Bailey's also had wild-flower fields on their acreage. Alex started spending most of her time in the flower fields with what she called imaginary friends while Brax would be playing at the treehouse with his school friends.

That summer boxelder bugs were really bad. The farmhouse was covered with them. Alex hated them. They were all over her bedroom windows and it creeped her out. She had problems falling asleep in that house because she felt like the bugs were going to get in and crawl all over her. She didn't want to be alone upstairs. Alex's parents assured her that the bugs would not get in her bed. Her parents would not allow her to go to bed with them or her brother, she needed to be in her own bed. Braxton could not stand hearing his sister cry up in her room so he would go up to her room and read her stories before bed or play music for her. She would drift off to sleep but as soon as he was gone, she would wake up.

She never felt comfortable upstairs by herself at nighttime. She told Braxton she felt like she was never really alone upstairs. She had a creepy feeling, it was the darkness, and she felt like monsters were in the upstairs with her. After she told Braxton how she felt, every night before bed, Braxton would turn on all the lights in every one of the rooms and walk with his sister in each room, looking in all the closets. He would try to comfort her by showing her nothing was there. Braxton started telling Alex stories about angels and how they were watching over her, protecting her from the darkness, when her brother could not be there, the angels would be there. Brax knew she was scared of those feelings, but he told her she needed to listen to those feelings. Her feelings are there to protect her, and when she feels those dark feelings, he told her to talk to the angels. He played her songs by Amy Grant and Michael W. Smith hoping that would calm her down and help her sleep. But every time he left the room, Alex would wake up.

Braxton begged his parents to let him switch rooms with his sister, but they would not allow it. They said they were not going to play that game. Whenever Alex cried about something Braxton would do anything for her, even move rooms if that's what she wanted. They were worried that Alex would change her mind after the switch and then beg to have the upstairs back. They were only going to be there for three more months. Alex was going to have to deal with it.

Alex said ten years must have gone by when Braxton revealed in a drunken mess that when they lived in the farmhouse, kids told him rumors about some foster kids that went missing on the Bailey's property. The kids joked to Braxton that the missing kids were probably buried somewhere on the farm. He didn't want to tell Alex about it while they were living there because he didn't want to freak her out any more than she already was, but he did tell his mom and dad. They laughed at Braxton saying it was a small town and kids their age like to make up stories to scare the new kids. They told him not to mention it to his sister.

Alex laughed, a little embarrassed, and shared with Keira that her sleep had been shit ever since the farmhouse. She also couldn't stand listening to Amy Grant and Michael W. Smith, she thought Type O Negative and Marilyn Manson were more soothing and laughed some more.

Alex told Keira that Darius knew all about her sleeping issues. He would brush her hair every night before bed, and usually, that would help relax her. Unfortunately, there were still times where she would be restless and Darius would tell her they should listen to tunes, eat some popcorn and play darts until she was ready to crash. Many times, in the middle of the night, they would go to their basement, pop some popcorn, listen to some David Gray and play darts and sometimes they would dance until morning. Alex told Keira that marrying Darius was the best thing that ever happened to her. She said it was like having a permanent sleepover with her best friend that made her heart skip a beat every time he walked in the room. When he looked at her, it affected her in such a way. She still couldn't believe he chose her. She just loved being in his presence. Even though Darius's death was devastating to Alex, sharing their love story made her realize how lucky she was to have such a story to tell.

When Alex talked about love that's when Keira swore she would never go down that path again. Keira's husband was her best friend too and she felt like her world was gone when they got a divorce. Everything she knew was gone. It was like a death to her. It was too painful. Alex understood completely and said, "Yeah thank goodness for the rabbit, am I right?" Keira looked at her confused and said, "What do you mean?" Alex repeated herself and said, "You know the vibrator, or any vibrator, it doesn't have to be the rabbit, any animal works." She laughed, "I also like the butterfly, dolphin, and the hummingbird," she laughed again. Keira looked at Alex and started laughing saying she was too old for that kind of thing. Alex was taken back, "Too old to have an orgasm? You are never too old for that. It's good for you. It's healthy. That's it, it's settled I'm getting you a rabbit. What's your favorite color?" Keira just laughed at her. Alex thought to herself, if she doesn't answer me, I am getting her a Vikings purple-colored rabbit. Keira never responded and was probably hoping Alex would forget about it, but she didn't.

Chapter 11

At the next happy hour Alex came baring gifts. She purchased a purple rabbit and some motion lotions for her good friend, wrapped them in a cute little gift bag. Alex gave Keira the gift bag and told her not to open it up until she got home. She didn't want her opening it up at the bar. Keira looked at her, with a weird look on her face. Alex just said, "Trust me, you're going to love it."

Alex shared with Keira that she lost her virginity at age 16. She told her about her first time and how disappointing it was. She thought the boy was nice, he knew it was her first time, so he was trying to be gentle, but it still hurt. She didn't understand what the big fuss was about. She would rather make out than have sex. She had sex multiple times and with multiple people and she was pretty sure she never had an orgasm. One day she asked her best friend Anika, who had been in a serious relationship, and who was always having sex and blabbing to Alex about it, what an orgasm felt like? Anika looked at her shocked and told her if she had to ask, she hasn't had one. She asked Alex if she ever masturbated. Alex was flabbergasted. No, she never masturbated, she would burn in hell for doing something like that, it was bad enough she was having promiscuous pre-marital sex. Anika told her she needed to get a vibrator.

Since Anika and Alex were underage, they had to wait until Anika's friend, who worked at the Adult Store, was working so the girls could go into the shop. Anika and Alex had to wait two days and then it was adult shop day. Alex was nervous and excited. She walked into the store and it was like a kid in a candy store. She saw so many pretty toys, lingerie, lotions, potions, oils, and S&M chairs and gadgets, books, and videos; she could have spent all week in that store. She wanted to know what everything was and how it was used. Alex lit up. Anika's friend told Alex she needed to start with the rabbit as a vibrator. There was a variety of colors and different sizes, and each one had something unique about it. There were some that had pearl beads up the shaft that rotated to change the texture and pressure, some had warming agents when they turned on it warmed up. There were glow-in-the-dark vibrators and multiple speed vibrators and some that came with removable attachments. Alex went with a hot pink rabbit that had pearl beads in the shaft. Anika's friend gave Alex two boxes of batteries, lubricant, and instructions on how to use it.

Alex was nervous about bringing home her new purchases. If Psycho Sharon busted her with any of that stuff she would have been beaten to a pulp. She had to hide them in her backpack and sneak into her room and lock the door. Alex said she put on some music. She could not wait to try the rabbit out. She thought for sure it would be a waste of time, she was positive Anika made up what an orgasm felt like or if women even got them. Alex took off her pants and panties, laid in bed. She put two batteries in the rabbit and took out the lubricant. The lubricant smelt like sweet coconut, she put a little on her vagina and a little on the rabbit, then she turned on the rabbit and placed it down by her vagina. She liked how it felt, she was aroused. She started getting warm and within seconds her body started shaking and she finally had an orgasm. When it was over, she was sweaty, flushed and her heart was racing. She took all her clothes off and made the rabbit do that seven more times. She thought to herself, "Anika is a genius!"

Alex told Anika that she wanted to go back to the adult store again. So, they did. Alex bought a lot more stuff. She became obsessed with pleasing herself. She really didn't care if she ever had sex with another person again.

After her first night with the rabbit, Alex began to read books on sex. She read more and learned more, and she wanted more. She read and saw videos about oral sex, and she wanted to try that too. For that, she needed another person. Alex told Keira about her quest to find the perfect person to have oral sex with. Alex said she was friends with this guy in her neighborhood; his name was Dom, short for Dominic. After he graduated from high school he went into the Marines. When he came home on holiday, Alex noticed that he ran every morning around 6:30. Alex got up one morning and went out for a run just before 6:30 and she "accidentally" ran into Dom. He was about 5'10, very muscular, dark complexion, with dark hair and dark eyes. Alex thought he was gorgeous and that the marines did him good. His body looked bigger and stronger. He carried himself straighter and with more confidence.

Alex and Dom chatted for a while. Dom told her he was going to be in town for another few weeks but then he was going back to Fort Myers, Florida. Alex enjoyed catching up with him and asked him if it would be ok if she ran with him while he was in town. She enjoyed the company and she needed the motivation. In a flirtatious way, he said it would be a privilege to run with her.

The next morning, Dom ran to Alex's house and Dom and Alex went for their morning run. They talked about high school since Alex was in her last year. She told him how she hated it. They talked about the same creeps, and how they were still creeps. They talked about the Marines and how much Dom liked the brotherhood, the opportunity to see other places, other countries, and support and defend the USA. Alex was impressed by how sincere he was. She knew he meant what he said. Dom wasn't just saying it because he thought he should. She admired him.

Dom ended up asking her more things about her, like where she was working, if she was going to go to college, what her plan was. She told him that she was working at the YMCA, loved the access to the pool and work-out facility. The Y was very flexible with her school hours. She worked there for four years and they promoted her to be a key person, which basically meant she could collect money, create memberships, and lock up the money and building at the end of the night. She said she was planning on getting a business degree. He asked her if she was interested in a specific business. She laughed at him and sheepishly said she really liked Adult toys. She thought adult stores got a bad rap, she thought there was a stigma around adult stores, people worried that someone will see them walking in or by the store, but she said, "Let's be honest everyone is interested about what is in an adult store." She thought people had a misconceived perception that all the things in an adult store were perverse. But she looked at the adult store as a place of learning more about one-self, and what you are into. There are many items in the store that help couples rekindle their desire for each other, creating a healthy sex life and fantasy, there's a variety of stuff that can help people enjoy sex and enjoying it with a partner, why is that perverted? She felt people needed to be educated more about sex, the health benefits, and be encouraged to try new things. She didn't think she should walk into a business program saying that though. Dom laughed and said, "Why not? You seem passionate about it, and obviously, you see a need. Are you thinking about being a sex consultant or something?" He said with a smile.

She liked being able to talk to Dom about her thoughts on the sex store and he didn't make fun of her. He asked her if she tried a lot of stuff out and she mentioned she had a nice collection. She admitted she read a lot of books on sex. She had a huge selection on Kama Sutra which educates and equips individuals on how to create and engage in luxury romance, intimacy, foreplay, sexual positions, the female and male orgasm, living well, the nature of love, and taking care of your love life. Dom looked at her with a surprised face and asked her if she had a boyfriend. She laughed and said no, she just liked reading about all of that stuff. It was interesting to her. Mainly because she was always taught that sex was a sin and dirty and she needed to stay away from it unless she was married, but even then, it should never be something a woman should enjoy. He looked at her and said, "Well, that's bullshit." Alex laughed and said, "Tell me about it. Welcome to my world." She then asked Dom if he had a girlfriend or a boyfriend? He said he didn't have either but if she was wondering, he liked girls in that way, not boys. Alex then looked at him and asked him if he ever had oral sex before. He laughed and confessed he had, he asked her if she had. She shook her head no and said that is one thing she would like to experience and hasn't yet. She doesn't have a boyfriend and doesn't see one in her near future any time soon.

Dom shrugged his shoulders and said, "Someday you'll get that chance and the guy will be very lucky, you being all read up on it and all." She looked at Dom, and said, "Would it be weird if we did?" Dom looked at her confused, "If we had oral sex? Like together?" She looked a bit embarrassed and said, "Yeah, like together. Are you attracted to me?" He laughed, "Yeah Alex, I'm a guy, who wouldn't be attracted to you? Plus, you talk about sex all day, so then I think about sex all day. Yes, I am attracted to you, but don't you think you should do that with someone you care about? Oral sex is very intimate." Alex looked at Dom and said, "I care about you. We just aren't together like that, but I'd totally have sex with you. You're hot! Plus, I want to try oral sex. You're my friend, and I'd rather be intimate with a friend than some stranger I just met at a party."

Dom looked at Alex like she was nuts, "Are you serious? Or are you playing with me?" Alex laughed, "I'm serious. Let's meet tomorrow. My parents work all day. Be at my place by 8:00 and shower before you come over." He looked at her and said, "Seriously?" Alex looked at him and said, "Yes, Dom! Seriously!" and she smiled as if she was a 6-year-old kid that got a brand-new bike for Christmas.

Dom showed up at Alex's house right at 8:00. Alex opened the door and grabbed him by the hand and took him upstairs to her room. She had some music playing in the background, Enigma, and had candles lit. She had oils sitting out. She shut her bedroom door and told him to take off his clothes as she took hers off. He looked nervous. She watched him take off his jeans, his boxers, and his t-shirt. He was ripped. He had that indented v-shape that she saw in magazines and the movies but never saw in the flesh. She was starting to feel flushed, her vagina was getting warm, she slid off her panties and then her sports bra. He just stared at her. He still looked nervous. She pushed him down on her bed, he was lying flat on his back. She sat on her bed and leaned in to kiss him on the lips and then started kissing his neck. His cock was hard. He had a nice size one too. She kept on kissing him and then said she wanted to try some flavored oil, so she explained that she was going to start with massaging him. He said ok as he nodded his head. She poured oil on her hand and started massaging his arms, neck, stomach, and went down to his cock, and massaged it a little bit then continued down his legs to his feet and when she was at the bottom of his feet she started sensually licking his foot, then she moved up his leg, then to his cock and balls. Then she licked up and down his cock as she played with his balls, she then started stroking his cock with her hand, as she was sliding him in and out of her mouth. He started tensing up and then, his legs and pelvis started jerking, he let out a loud moan as he came in her mouth. She kept sucking until he was all done. She read it was disrespectful to spit. She didn't think it tasted bad. It was warm and a little salty, but she also tasted the massage oil; it was a strawberry flavor so that could have helped. She liked his reaction. She liked knowing she could excite him with her mouth. For her, that was the challenge. Alex looked at Dom and said, "What did you think?" with a smile. Dom looked at her in an erotic daze and said, "You have never done that before? You only read about it? Alex, I have never experienced something like that, and I have had oral sex before. You were amazing."

Dom sat up and kissed Alex. He rolled her over on her back and he copied everything she did with the massage oil. He started massaging her neck, her arms, her breasts, her stomach, down to her lady parts but just brushed over them, he went down her legs to her feet, and once he was at the bottom of her feet he started dragging his tongue sensually up her body. He stopped at her lady parts and kissed it, he opened his mouth and he kissed it with his tongue. Then he came up from between her legs and dragged his tongue up her stomach to her breasts, he licked her nipples and massage her breasts. He then continued to kiss her, and he dragged his tongue back down to her vagina. He opened her legs up wider and put his face right in her flower, she opened up for him and he moved his tongue, back a fourth, sucking sometimes, but mostly licking fast, so fast like her rabbit. She was moaning and arching her back. She started convulsing and cried out, "Oh my God!" She came all over. He stayed down there as her flower pulsated. He continued to lick and kiss but more gently. Then he moved his head up and kissed her body moving up to her face. He rolled beside her with his arm around her. He kissed her on her cheek. She said nothing for a while. Then he said, "How was that?" She said, "What did they teach you in the Marine Corps? Good God Baby, you have been blessed with one hell of an amazing tongue." Dom laughed.

Dom and Alex laid on her bed naked, resting for a while listening to Enigma, and then Alex said, "Have you ever done the 69 position?" He said he did try it once. He asked her if she wanted to try it out. She nodded her head and he said, "Ok, do you want to be on top or bottom?" She laughed and said both. He laughed and said, "Let's start with me being on bottom, that might be more comfortable for you since I'm bigger." She nodded in agreement. They moved into that position and started performing on each other when all-of-a-sudden Alex's bedroom door opened. It was Alex's mom. Dom jumped up quickly and tried to get his clothes on but ended up giving up, he just picked them all up from the floor as Alex's mom said, "I think you better go." He looked scared shitless at Alex and said, "Bye." He ran out of that house so fast. Alex's mom picked up the first thing she saw, which was the family dog's knotted-up, rag bone. And beat Alex with it, up and down her body, calling her a whore, slut, and the devil's temptress. Alex crossed her arms over her head and face and curled in the fetal position as she was being beaten. The beating left welts all over Alex's body. Sharon had hit Alex before, but nothing like that. Alex's whole body was stinging. She had a hard time sitting, walking, and laying down, all of it was so painful, but nothing was as painful as seeing the hate that was all over her mom's face as she was getting wailed on. Alex was forbidden to leave her house and she was absolutely not allowed to see Dom even when he came over to say he was going back to Florida.

Alex talked to Keira at length about sex and how religion and society painted the picture that sex is dirty. But she didn't think it was. It was a natural human instinct. It's how we were created. She went into great detail about what an orgasm does to the brain and how it releases chemicals into the body that gives a person that euphoric feeling. That's a great thing. It helps stabilize mood and your immune system. She started laughing and realized Keira obviously knew all of that, she worked in neurology back in the day. Maybe she just needed a reminder and the rabbit would be a good reminder.

Alex bragged about being the one who helped her brother and sister-in-law get pregnant with their first baby, maybe the 2nd, 3rd, and 4th too, ha. Braxton and Desirae were having problems getting pregnant, they tried for many years. Desirae went to a couple of Alex's sex toy parties, but she was always pretty shy about talking about sex. Braxton was her first and only boyfriend, her first and only everything. She never even kissed another boy. All she knew was Braxton. Alex of course felt bad for her, she thought everyone should 'taste the rainbow' before they settle down. Taste the rainbow meant to taste test what was out there, know what you like before you go all in, and lock it in. But not tasting the rainbow for Braxton and Desirae worked out for them, they were still married. However, they were going on year six and still haven't been able to get pregnant. Des had a couple of girlfriends that talked about Alex's sex toy parties and having one-on-one consults with her for advice. One friend needed help bringing romance back into the bedroom. Alex gave her a book on romance, role-playing, and fun date nights. She also gave her a few toys that worked great for couples and erotic lubricants to try out. Another friend consulted her about her pelvic floor. After she had kids, she had issues with tinkling, and she would sometimes just pee herself when she would do something without thinking like laugh or sneeze. Alex gave her a few ben wa balls, different sizes, and gave her instructions on how to use them. She also gave her a tightening cream that she could rub on her vagina. She told her she could try that before having sex, it should tighten up her vagina, it would make it feel small and tighter, giving her the feeling of what her vagina probably felt like before she had a 10-pound watermelon push through it.

One night Des confided in Alex and asked her for help. Alex was THRILLED. She felt that her mission in life was to release people of their sexual burdens. She wanted to help people learn more about sex, enjoy sex, even if it was just to pleasure themselves, sex was a magical thing and to experience a climax and orgasm is healing to the human body.

Des shared with Alex that she went to the doctors, nothing was wrong with her or Brax. However; they might have to go with artificial insemination if they wanted to get pregnant. Alex assured her that she could help with the problem. They were probably just so stressed about getting pregnant that it stopped them from getting pregnant. Stress can wreak havoc on the body, so stress needs to go. Alex told her to stop planning on the calendar when they were going to have sex, stop reminding Brax about it. Stop telling him the date and time they needed to have sex, stop trying complicated positions, stop doing that weird thing after sex when the lady holds her knees together in the air, in the fetal position hoping to direct the semen to the cervix. It's important to know when she's ovulating, but that's for her to figure out and keep to herself, telling Braxton just makes him all worked up and nervous. He wanted her to be happy and he knew she has wanted a baby forever and he wants to give that to her.

Alex went to one of her treasure chests. She had a shelf of multiple lubricants, lotions, and oils. She grabbed two bottles of oil. She handed them over to Des and said in a very serious voice, "You're going to seduce my brother." She had a sneaky devilish grin; she was having fun with this. "What you need to do is go home one night, plan to make a meal you both like, pour yourself a nice glass of red wine, get dressed in a sexy lingerie outfit, I say wear something red, and high heels." Desirae was part Indian, dot, not feather, as Alex would say. She was exotic-looking with dark skin, long black wavy hair, and big dark brown eyes. She thought her brother married the hottest woman in the world. Red was a color of power, seduction, and love. "Play some mood music in the background, something that makes YOU feel sexy. Start cooking and as you prepare the meal, drink your wine. When he comes home, he will be pleasantly surprised, but even more surprised with what you are wearing. Pour him a glass of Guinness, his favorite. Have him have a seat and serve him his meal. Whatever you do, do not give into him if he wants to jump your bones, not even if he begs for it. Make sure you both eat your meal. It will drive him nuts. After dinner is done, tell him you have some desert for him but first, you want him to change out of his work clothes. Let him know that you know he has been stressed and you want to give him a little body massage before dessert. Tell him to get naked on the bed. Rub the oil all over him, from top to bottom, slather him with the oil. It smells good, feels good and it's edible". She said with a grin. "Get the oil all over him, his back, legs, butt, balls, everywhere massage it in, it will feel sensual, the oil will warm as you rub it in, it won't get hot, it will be a comfortable warm and he will get excited, and so will you. Keep massaging him until he can't take it anymore, and then go get him, girl. You both will be all oiled up and it will feel amazing. Do what you feel like doing. Just enjoy it."

Eight weeks later Alex got a package at her door. It was a bottle of wine with a card announcing she was going to be an aunt. It looked like Des kissed the card, it was the shade of Red Passion, the color Des usually wears, and in Des's handwriting, it read, Thank you! I love you Sis! Alex teared up, smiled, and shouted out-loud, "YES! IT WORKED!"

Alex and Keira both had to take an Uber home that night. They had way too much to drink but their motto was, "They ain't eva had too much fun". Keira loved being around Alex. Alex made her feel young. They both decided they needed to have more happy hours, at least once a month if not more, it was good for them.

Chapter 12

Dr. Heart

Alex and Keira did happy hours at least twice a month if not more. It was always at the same place, Oscar's. About seven months into their happy hours, Alex and Keira decided to meet at Oscar's on a Friday night. Oscar's was hopping. Keira and Alex were at their usual table, drinking their usual drinks, laughing and people watching. They liked to make up stories of why people were there. Alex was impressed with some of the stuff Keira came up with. She was such a witty and creative woman. Maybe it was from reading all those Housekeeping Magazines, she thought to herself.

Jeff came to the table and delivered two more drinks. He looked at Keira and then at Alex and said, "The gentleman at the bar bought these for you, two lovely ladies." He winked and walked away. Alex looked at Keira and said, "Which gentleman at the bar? The bar is packed." Alex laughed and she and Keira raised their glasses to the bar to say thank you to whoever bought them the drinks and they smiled. They both laughed and kept drinking. Keira was telling Alex that she was going to be out of town for a couple of days. Her crazy sister-in-law was having surgery and she needed to help her brother take care of her. She loved her brother. He was so good to her. Alex met him a couple of times. He was a great guy but yeah, his wife was fruitier than a box of fruit loops. Keira asked Alex if she would be willing to swing in and check up on her cats for her while she was gone. Alex had no problem doing that of course, she had nothing else going on. She didn't do much on the weekends, she usually worked out, did laundry, house chores, and sometimes she went out to small local bars to catch a band, but other than that her life was pretty boring. Alex told Keira she was thinking about going back to school to finish her business degree. She only needed to finish five more classes. She stopped going to school when Darius died. She couldn't function, but now she thought she could get back into it. She smiled at Keira and said, "What do you say Sex Kitten, should we get that brothel started?" They both laughed.

Alex was still laughing but Keira stopped. Keira was looking behind Alex and her eyes grew big. So, Alex turned around to see what Keira was looking at. A guy was walking in their direction. He was probably one of the best-looking guys Alex had seen in a while. He looked like he just walked out of a GQ magazine. Her radar has been turned off for almost two years now, she never thought twice about checking anyone out, but this guy, um….she was checking out. He looked like he could be 28 or 30 years old, at least 6'4, lean, wearing a black suit, white dress shirt, with the top two buttons of his shirt unbuttoned. Alex thought his tie must be in his car, he probably came straight from work, like her, stopped to have a couple, and then head home. He was still walking and then walked straight to their table. He had a super sexy smile, he seemed confident but relaxed. He had a surfer boy haircut, short in the back but the front was a little longer, it was a sandy blonde color, and he had amazing steel blue eyes. He was gorgeous. He was smiling as if he knew them, he opened his mouth and said "I apologize; I didn't mean to interrupt your conversation I just wanted to come by and say hi. I am new to the area and I stop off at this bar often. I see you two here a lot. Usually, I'm always bellied up at the bar. I shouldn't say always, I'm not an alcoholic or anything." He laughed, then he laughed some more. It was super adorable. He had a cute European accent. "I assumed the two of you were mother and daughter, I thought it was sweet that you had such a good relationship, so I had the bartender send over some drinks. But now I see, (he turned and looked straight at Keira) that you are way too young to be her mother." Keira laughed. Alex laughed. Oh, he was smooth. Keira ended up inviting him to sit down with them, so he pulled up a chair.

They found out that he recently moved there from Florida, but he was born and raised in the UK. He was a cardiologist. He finished all his med school, residency, and fellowships in Florida. He was offered a consultant job at the same hospital the girls worked at. The girls tried to convince him that the Minnesota winters weren't as bad as the movies like Fargo made it out to be. They laughed. He was going to freeze his ass off.

The girls had a great time chatting it up with the heart doctor. He stayed and visited with them for about an hour. Jeff came by to see if they needed any more drinks. Keira was getting tired, so she asked for her bill. Jeff responded that the table was paid up and wished them all a safe and good night. Keira looked at the good doctor and said, "Did you get our tab?" He shrugged his shoulders and said it was the least he could do. They were so polite in asking him to join them on their girl's night out.

Kiera and Alex thanked him for taking care of the bill and said they hoped to see him again, which might be a good possibility since they all frequent there. He offered to walk them out. They left the bar waving and saying goodbye one last time to the bartenders. Keira's car was parked in the front, in a handicapped parking space, so as soon as they were out the door she was basically at her car. She turned and looked at the doctor, thanked him again, and wished him goodnight and good luck with his new job. She turned to Alex and hugged her tight saying she would call her tomorrow to remind her about the cats, and then she whispered in Alex's ear, he is a heart doctor, he fixes hearts for a living. She kissed her on her cheek. Alex blushed; she knew what Keira was hinting at. She kissed Keira back on the cheek and told her that she loved her. Keira said she loved her too and they would talk tomorrow. They waved goodbye.

Alex lived a little further away and thought she better get an Uber. She looked at the doctor and said she was going to call an Uber and went on to say it was nice meeting him and wished him a good night. He glanced over at her and said, "Alex, I don't have anything else going on tonight, nothing going on tomorrow, do you want to hang some more, or do you need to be heading home too? I only live five minutes away from here we could go to my place and have some wine, talk some more, find something on Netflix?" Alex was caught off guard and didn't know what to say. He laughed as he shook his head "Did that sound stupid? You don't even know me, I could be a serial killer, why would you want to come over to a stranger's house to drink and watch Netflix?" Alex laughed but she thought about it and she didn't want to go home. He seemed like a nice guy and if he ended up being a serial killer, oh shit. She looked at him and shrugged her shoulders, "It's better than me going home and doing all that by myself. Sure, I'll come hang with you for a bit." He looked at her with his steel-blue eyes and sexy smile and said, "Great! My car is right here." It was a silver Audi R8 sports car. Fucking hot, just about as hot as he was. He opened the passenger's side door for her.

She commented saying how nice his car was. She told him that it still had that new car smell. He nodded and told her that it was fairly new; he hadn't spent much time in it, so luckily his car didn't have his funky smell yet. He and Alex laughed. Alex spoke up and told him she actually liked the smell of Armani. He looked at her with a surprising look and she said, "Aren't you wearing Acqua Di Gio by Armani? He nodded and said with a smile, "Great guess, Great nose." She smiled and said it was one of her favorite smells.

The doctor turned on the car and music started playing. The music sounded so good. Some songs she had never heard before, mixes and match-ups of songs she had never heard before. The music mix had all the perfect ebb and flows. She asked him about it, and he told her that he had a good buddy that he went to med school with that was a mix doctor. After long nights of studying they needed an outlet to get their mind off of books and school, so his buddy Levi would host underground rave parties. Levi would DJ for fun.

One night, some club owner from Miami ended up at one of Levi's parties and offered him to come out to his club and spin some records. Levi jumped at the opportunity. The DJ system and equipment at a high-end club would be killer to check out. Levi, the heart doctor, and a couple of their other friends went to check out the club. The club had heightened energy, people dancing from wall to wall, it was exhilarating. When Levi got introduced as a guest DJ, the crowd cheered. Levi got up in the DJ booth and started doing his thing. Levi was in his element. The hype and energy was unstoppable. It was like the music elevated and levitated the crowd. The heart doctor and his friends had never witnessed something like that before. It was crazy and exciting to watch their friend work a crowd like that. That night Levi got offered a permanent DJ gig with that club and the other two clubs the owner had. Levi dropped out of med school and jumped at the offer. Levi told the guys there was no better feeling than spinning records and watching the crowd, jump, and dance, screaming his name. He would never get that feeling being a medical doctor. The doctor said Levi often sends him his new mixes and that's what they were listening to, it was called 'Levi's Late Night Drive Playlist'.

They showed up at the doctor's place literally five minutes later. Alex was a little bummed the drive was over; she loved being in his car, watching him talk about his friend, and listening to the music. It was so fresh and exciting. He lived in the brand-new condos that were built within the last year. His condo was very modern, all shades of grey, and spotless. She couldn't believe he just moved there a few months ago, she would still be living out of her boxes. Maybe he had professional movers and cleaners do all of it for him. Then she thought the hospital probably paid for it all.

He watched Alex as she looked around his place. She turned and looked at him with a busted look and then told him how nice of a place it was. He nodded and said thanks and that he liked it. He obviously liked nice things. It intimidated her. He started rattling off different kinds of wine, and then he stopped and said he had a variety of other alcoholic beverages too, and then laughed promising her he was not an alcoholic and offered non-alcoholic beverages too. She laughed and asked him if he had captain, he nodded. She said she would take a Captain diet if he had diet coke. He said perfect, he would make himself the same thing. She watched him make the drinks, and then she confessed that she really didn't care if he was an alcoholic. They both laughed. He gave her the drink. Even his glassware was cool and modern. She had never been around someone like him before, it was super exciting but then she started getting nervous. She thought what the hell am I doing here? I don't know this dude. As she was panicking in her head, he asked her if they should pick something to watch or if they should just visit and listen to music? She went with watching something because she didn't know if, at some point, they might not have anything to talk about and she might find herself awkwardly staring at him while listening to music.

He asked her what kind of movies she was into. She said action, crime movies, or psychological thrillers. He seemed shocked. She laughed and wanted to know why he was so surprised. He just said he would have picked her out to be a comedy girl, maybe romantic comedy? And she tilted her head and said, "Is that because that's what most girls like? Baby, I ain't like most girls." He looked stunned when she called him baby. He smiled. He noticed she was done with her drink and offered her another one. She said, "Of course, and thank you, cause, I am actually an alcoholic." They both laughed.

He handed her a fresh drink, she sat down on his very new-looking, light grey, big comfy couch. He dimmed the lights and sat close to her but not too close. They looked through the Netflix options and ended up on an oldie but a goodie, *The Departed*. She saw it many times, but it had been years, he had seen it once or twice before too. It was a good choice, if they ended up talking through most of the movie, she wouldn't feel bad since he's seen it before, and if they ended up sitting there watching the movie, at least it was a decent movie.

He started the movie and then realized he was still in his work clothes. So was Alex. He asked her if it was ok for him to change, and she said sure. He offered her to change in more comfortable clothes and then laughed. She was basically wearing PJs, scrubs are so comfy, but she wore them all day and she felt like she wreaked of hospital. She would love to get out of her scrubs so she asked him, "Um, what would you suggest?" He said he had t-shirts, sweatshirts, sweatpants, he didn't know why he said pants, there is no way she could wear his pants, he was so tall, and she was so petite.

He went into his bedroom to change and walked out wearing a pair of grey, yes grey, Nike sweatpants, and a white Ron Jon Surf t-shirt, he also had a dark grey, yes grey, Gold Coast surf t-shirt in his hand. He showed it to Alex and said it was an older one and a little snug on him so maybe she could try it. She laughed and told him no, maybe he should quick, put it on so she could see how snug it was. He threw it at her and laughed. She could tell she was feeling a little more comfortable. Even though he was a doctor and obviously liked the finer things in life, he was not a stuck-up prick. He actually seemed sweet, sensitive, and funny, really funny. He asked her if she wanted another drink. She was done already with her 2nd. She nodded, shrugged her shoulders, and said, "Sure, why not?" He smiled and made both of them another drink. She asked where the bathroom was. She thought she better change in the bathroom; it was more proper.

The bathroom was elegant, but grey, yes, grey. It had multiple colors of grey tile everywhere. The bathroom was massive. She could totally sleep in his jacuzzi bathtub. It looked like a souped-up hot tub. He also had a shower room. A full room dedicated to showering in his bathroom. His towels were big, soft, fluffy, GREY towels. She thought grey was a colorless color, a safe color. Then she stopped during mid-thought, "Shit, I better hurry and change my shirt. How long have I been in here? He probably thinks that I'm snooping again, or worse he might think I took a shit." She was telling herself to focus and change the damn shirt. She took off her scrub shirt and her underneath long-sleeve t-shirt. She looked in the mirror and laughed and mouthed to herself, *What the fuck am I doing?* She put his grey Gold Coast shirt on. It was still pretty big but it was fine. It smelt clean, like Tide. She walked out of the bathroom. He smiled at her and he said, "You look great. You feel ok?" She nodded and thought to herself *yep, he thinks I took a huge dooker in his pretty bathroom, nice.*

She sat back on the couch and he handed her, her drink. She thanked him and took a couple of sips and then asked him if he was a surfer. He had surf t-shirts and he had a surf boy haircut. She asked him where his surfboard was? She smiled. He said, "I enjoy surfing but I probably won't get too many chances to do it in Minnesota though, huh?" They laughed. They watched a little of the movie and talked about his time in Florida, but he really didn't want to talk about med school, he said he didn't want to bore her. He asked her questions about her and her work. She told him that she worked in the outpatient setting of the clinic. She has worked there for 12 years. His eyes got big and asked her if she started when she was 12? What a charmer she thought. He smiled. He wanted to know her dreams and he seemed genuinely interested in her and wanted to get to know her. She told him she was still working on her bachelor's degree in business, seems like it was taking forever. She started and stopped multiple times for different reasons, but didn't mention why specifically, she just said life happens. He nodded his head. She asked him why and when he knew he wanted to be a doctor. He said it was a family thing; he came from a long line of doctors, all cardiologists. He said he was sorry for not having a more meaningful answer than it was the "family business."

The conversation moved on quickly to tattoos. He asked her if she had any tattoos. She said no, but she liked tattoos on the right people. She thought her body was too small and petite to have a tattoo unless it was something very small. She liked tattoos but for her, they had to have meaning. She thought about it a lot actually. If she got a tattoo, she would get the words 'feel the feels' tattooed on the inside of her right bicep. She explained that it was to remind her not to walk through life numb, and then she lifted up her glass of captain and looked at it and said, "It's still a work in progress." She said she wouldn't mind getting a tattoo of an angel and a star. When she was younger, she always had a hard time getting to sleep. In an attempt to help her fall asleep, her brother would make up all kinds of nighttime stories to tell her before bed. Her favorite one was about angels that were at war. Her brother explained that there were good and bad angels, and during one heated battle between the good and bad angels, one good angel got badly hurt. Her left wing was broken, she tried to fly up to heaven to get it fixed. She was having a hard time flying because her wing was so badly hurt.

A bright star in the sky saw the beautiful angel and wanted to help her. The star came down to the angel and took her by the wing and brought her up to heaven. After that, Alex was obsessed with stars and thought angels and stars should always be together. Embarrassed that she told him the story she laughed, "I know it must sound stupid, but yeah, if I got tatted, I'd want a star somewhere, and I would probably have to get an angel too. I hear getting inked is very addicting." She laughed some more. Then she asked him if he had any tattoos. He said he didn't, not because he didn't like them though. He said unlike her he had no clue what he would get or where. He also wasn't opposed to getting one; he just didn't have anything in mind, nothing that meant something strong enough for him to permanently put it on his body. Alex told him he could get a heart tattoo since he was a heart doctor, or better yet he could get a heart tattooed on him every time he fixed someone's heart. He laughed and told her his body would be covered, otherwise, he wouldn't be a very successful cardiologist. Then he looked at her very sweetly and said, "Maybe, one day I will get a heart tattoo to resemble the heart I won?" Alex just gave him a thoughtful nod. The movie was over, and it was late. Alex told him she should probably order an Uber and go. She asked him if she could use the bathroom one last time. He smiled and nodded his head.

He turned on some music while she was in the bathroom. The music was light, almost erotic, definitely mood music. It sounded so pleasing to the ear, very relaxing. This time she was in and out of the bathroom quickly. She walked out of the bathroom smelling her hands. She loved the smell of his soap. He noticed her smelling her hands and said, "The scent is Coconut Lime Verbena, my sister got me hooked on it." Alex said, "Yeah, it smells super good. You have a sister? Is she a cardiologist too?" He laughed and said, "No, she didn't go into the family business, she and her husband deal with real estate and property development of high-priced condos and resorts all over the country." Alex thought that explains it, his sister probably showed him how to decorate his place to look "show" ready all the time. Maybe this was one of their properties? He went on to say they live in New York. Alex just nodded her head.

Alex asked about the music that was playing. She told him it was titillating. He smiled and told her it was one of Levi's Late Night music mixes, one of his favorites to chill out to. She smiled and said it was really good. She got her phone out and was starting to order an Uber. He stood up and got close to her, touching her hand, and said, "Hey, hey" while she was messing with her phone, "...um you don't have to leave, you can stay over. I have two furnished bedrooms. I can drop you off at your car in the morning or whenever. It's late don't get in an Uber now." She looked at him and laughed, "Dude! I'm feeling so gross now," he looked taken back and hurt by what she said, and then realizing what she said, she corrected the statement saying, "No, No, Baby." And when she called him baby, she could tell it affected him, in a good way, he liked being called baby. "I feel gross because I need to shower. I don't want to mess up your super amazing grey sheets." She laughed, she could not believe she said that out loud. Watch his sheets were the only thing at his place that wasn't grey. He laughed and said, "Yeah, there's a lot of greys, you can thank my sister for that too." Alex wanted to jump up and down and say she knew it, but doing it in her head would have to suffice. Alex just nodded. Then he looked at her and said, "Stay if you want to stay, take a shower if you want to, it's totally ok with me or you can go.... it's just late to get an Uber. There are crazy people out there, and now I am over my limit to drive you, otherwise, I would. I am not trying to be a dirt-bag, honestly. I'll be a perfect gentleman. You can shower, have your own room and everything." He looked tired. She could tell he was getting exhausted trying to convince her that he wasn't a serial killer or anything and that he was actually a nice, respectful guy.

Alex looked at him, put her phone down, and asked him if he had an extra phone charger because her battery was running low. If anything, she wanted to make sure she had enough juice in her phone in case he ended up being a serial killer and needed to call for help. She laughed to herself. He showed her the charging pad on the kitchen island and also gave her another phone charger she could take into the spare bedroom if she wanted her phone closer to her. She looked at him and thought, *God, he is so fucking hot and he has his shit together. Smooth Mother Fucker.*

She looked up at him and said, "What if I don't want you to be?" He looked at her confused, and said "What?" She said, "What if I don't want you to be a gentleman, baby?" He did a double-take and he smiled, this time Alex saw his dimples, fuck he was cute. He said, "Try calling me baby one more time and you might find out." She got excited and nervous, it was a challenge, she looked at him and said, "Baby" in a sultry voice and he pounced. He had her up in the air so fast, she wrapped her legs around him and he kissed her. It was passionate. They continued to kiss, and he carried her into his bedroom. She felt as if they were flying. She knew she was small and weighed like 100 pounds, but he seemed super strong, he flung her around like she was a sack of potatoes. She was shocked and turned the fuck on.

He laid her down on the bed and kissed her more deeply. He tasted good. He grabbed her arms and placed them above her head, and he intertwined his fingers in between hers. She just kept thinking, *this guy is so big he literally touching every part of my body.* His whole body was stretch over hers, even with her arms up over her head. He smelt so good. He let go of her hands and cuffed her face in his hands. His hands were so huge, they were soft and gentle. He gazed into her eyes and said, "Is this ok? Should we stop?" She just had enough in her to say, "NO! Don't stop... please don't stop." Was she begging? Holy crap! She was begging. She hasn't had this much excitement in 17 months, don't fucking stop. He kissed her more passionately. She could feel his cock poking her underneath his sweatpants and it felt big and strong. He was moving up and down her, dry humping her. She started moaning. She couldn't handle it. The begging and moaning started to increase substantially. He took his shirt off and his arms were fucking ripped. The dude seriously works out. She looked down his body and he had an 8 or 10 pack, it looked like muscle on muscle, his v-shape was so defined she thought for sure it was from all the surfing he did. He kept sweeping his hair out of his eyes so he could look into hers. He started kissing her neck and ears. It was like he was a kid in a candy shop. She felt desired and sexy. He moved his hair again, and said: "That's it, I'm getting a fucking haircut tomorrow." That was the first time she heard him swear and it sounded so hot with his accent. He rolled over on his back and lifted her up and placed her on top of him. She took off her shirt, well his shirt that she was wearing, and threw it. She was wearing a navy-blue laced bra, she looked down and thought thank God it was a pretty bra, not one of those tan old lady bras. He looked at her with a lustful look. She could tell he liked what he saw. She unfastened and took off her bra. He sat up and kissed her, then kissed her neck, he went down to her breasts and passionately kissed them. He licked her nipples and gently tugged at them with his lips. It felt amazing. He felt amazing.

He started pulling at her scrub pants trying to get them to roll down, she could tell he was frustrated, and through the bulge, in his sweatpants, she knew he wanted more. She was feeling warmth in between her legs, that good warmth. Her flower was starting to swell. She slid off him and dropped her pants. She was wearing matching navy blue laced booty shorts, once again she was super pleased that they were a decent pair of panties. She had a great ass. She knew it. She worked hard on it. Her ass looked the best in little booty shorts. They accentuated her round, firm little ass. He checked her out. His eyes full of excitement, he reached out for her and lifted her on top of him. She still had her booty shorts on, she glided up and down on him, she loved feeling his erection, rubbing up against her. It was so hard. She wanted it bad.

They kept kissing, she was breathing heavy, she could feel her heart racing. She asked him if he had condoms. He looked up at her like, 'Shit! Do I have condoms?' He got up quickly and went to his closet and came back out with a strip of condoms. He laughed and looked at her with confidence that they might actually go through all of them. As he walked to the bed, he pulled off his sweatpants. He was wearing white, Calvin Klein boxer briefs, and he looked fucking hot. She looked at his v-shape and pictured a heart tattoo and thought *ooo… that could be a perfect spot for a tat*. His cock was bulging in those briefs, poor dude needed to come out for air. He saw her looking. He looked back at her with the most lustful look. He licked his lips, and flipped his hair back away from his eyes, as he slid off his briefs. Holy shit. The man was beautiful, and his cock was HUGE! He grabbed her hand and placed it on him. Oh, she wanted it. She stroked it for a while, while he was kissing her, she honestly couldn't handle it anymore. She looked up at him, "Baby, I want you." That was all it took. He ripped off a condom from the strip. He got into the bed, flipped on his back, and rolled the condom on. He looked up at her with hungry eyes. She never dropped her panties so fast. She straddled him. They were kissing hard and fast. He was touching her everywhere. She was rubbing on him but didn't put him inside her yet, she wanted to wait just a few seconds more; she liked seeing him so excited.

Usually, Alex thought of her vagina as a flower. When she got excited it would swell, like a flower coming to life, the petals would get bigger and fluff out, she would get wet like a fresh dew mist, but tonight she thought of her vagina as a venus flytrap. She was aggressive, and if his cock came close to her opening, she was going to swallow it. She rocked some more and then she placed him inside her. Oh my GOD, he was so big, so hard, and he felt so amazing. She was so wet. She rode on him, gliding up and down. He was moaning, telling her how good she felt. She watched him as he was looking intently at her as if he was studying her as if he was waiting for her to cum, did he want to see her expression? She continued to ride up and down him. He was kissing and fondling her breasts, he glanced up at her and all of a sudden she hit her climax, she arched her back and continued to glide up and down his cock, she closed her eyes as she came. It felt like a volcanic gush as she came all over him. She screamed so loud, that sweet release was what she needed. Her vagina was pulsating. She teared up. It felt so good, but she felt so bad. She felt like she was betraying Darius. She opened her eyes and looked at the doctor. She was still gliding up and down on him. He stopped her from gliding, and he sat straight up, staying inside her. He looked concerned, he put his hands on her face, her face felt so small when he did that, he wiped her tears away with his thumb and asked her if she was ok, did he hurt her? She could understand why he would ask, he was a huge motherfucker, and she was crying. She looked at him and shook her head no, she grabbed his hand, and kissed the thumb that wiped her tears away, and then placed that thumb in her mouth and sucked on it, pulled it out and kissed it again and said, "No baby, you didn't hurt me, you feel amazing." She said that word again, and it excited him, he leaned up and kissed her pulling her close to him, and he flipped her around, rolling her on her back. He was now on top of her, still inside her, he gently, but deeply fucked her, she moaned, he moaned. He fucked her slow and deep, and she started cumming all over him again. She moaned with desire. She was feeling all the feels. And tears welled up in her eyes again. He looked at her and he slowed down to an almost stop. He asked her again if she was ok. Every time he asked her that, she felt more attracted to him. She thought it was so sweet that he was paying that much attention to her. He seemed genuine, kindhearted, and sensitive. She nodded her head and said she was more than ok, he was making her feel ALIVE. He smiled that big sexy smile again. He kissed her deeply and pushed himself deep into her again slowly, then again, slowly. They both moaned. She came again. This time she looked at his face while she was cumming. She wanted to look in his face as she came. He was so hot, and she could see how much he was enjoying being inside her. She felt complete ecstasy as she came and was looking into his eyes. He kissed her again and again, his face looked so serious, he kept pumping into her and moaning. He whispered in her ear, "Are you ready for me to come now? I don't think I can hold off any longer." He was breathing heavy and moaning. She thought *holy crap he was asking permission*? She was being so selfish, she took what she wanted, so should he. Her vagina was pulsating with excitement, just from him whispering in her ear. Every word he whispered made her flower tickle. It was as if he was able to touch every pleasure nerve in her body with that one whisper. She nodded her head giving him permission. He whispered in her ear again, "Tell me to come." She was like WHOA...... her venus flytrap was pulsating, and he was fucking her deeper and faster, and she moaned, finally she said it, "I want you to come inside me, baby." He let out a powerful moan, as he pumped in her two more times. The last pump he went so deep, she thought he would go right through her. He stopped pumping.

He waited a bit and then moved ever so gently, pulling out just a little, leaving himself in her, he slid his arm around her and lifted her up to bring her closer to him and pushed himself back in her completely. He moaned and whispered in her ear, "That's what happens when you call me baby." And he kissed her ear, her cheek, and then he kissed her on the mouth. He held her tight. He felt so strong, so amazing. He eventually backed away and pulled himself out of her. He got out of bed and offered her his hand. She took it. He smiled at her and said, "You still want that shower?"

He led her to the bathroom, and to the shower room. He opened the glass doors, Alex walked in, the walls were multi-colored grey tiled walls, there were three huge shower heads, one on each side of the room and one in the middle. He turned them all on. The showerheads had colored lights that seemed to be in sync with the music that was playing, the lights changed with the beat of the music. It was seriously the coolest thing she had ever seen. They went under separate shower heads, directly across from each other. They started washing she watched him washing his body. He was so sexy, she felt like she was in a dream. She started to wash her hair. He washed his hair, keeping his distance. She could see that he was getting hard looking at her wash herself, so she slowly walked over to him and started washing him, lathering up soap and rubbing it on his chest, his arms, his 10 pack, and then down to his massive cock. She started stroking it and then she gradually worked her way down, getting on her knees and she placed him in her mouth. She was wondering if she could even open up wide enough. He was long but he was ohhh so wide too. It wasn't easy but she did it, she was there for what seemed like seconds when he pulled her up and whipped her around, pressing her stomach up against the tiled wall, with his body pressed up against her back. With his left arm he grabbed both of her arms, raising them up over her head, he pressed his body up against her harder. She felt him, all of him. With his right hand he dragged two of his fingers down the right side of her body starting at the top of her right arm, he gradually dragged his fingers down her body as he passionately kissed the right side of her ear, neck, and back. He slid his right hand around her stomach and then slid it down to her vagina. With two of his fingers he started rubbing her clitoris, fast, he was way better than her rabbit, as he was touching her he whispered in her ear, "Alexandra, I could fuck you all night, you need to tell me when your little body needs a break." He kept rapidly playing with her clitoris and she started to moan, she started pulsating, she moaned louder with excitement and came. He turned her around to face him. He passionately kissed her and then said, "It's going to be hard to let you go." He backed away from her and said, "I'm going to make us something to eat. When you are ready to get out, there will be a robe hanging outside the shower for you. Take your time." He kissed her on the forehead and walked out grabbing a towel and wrapped it around his waist.

She eventually came out of the shower. She tried on the robe but it was ginormous on her so she decided to wrap herself in a towel. She sat down at his island and saw that he made scrambled eggs and ham. He also had fresh fruit on the side consisting of blueberries, strawberries, and cut-up bananas. He apologized saying he didn't have anything to make pancakes, otherwise he would have. She smiled and said, "No, this is great. I hardly ever get breakfast. Thank you so much." He asked her what she liked to eat in the morning, and she told him that she usually has yogurt in the morning during the week and then on the weekends usually a screwdriver or a bloody mary. She laughed. He said he had orange juice and offered to make her a screwdriver. She laughed and said she felt like maybe she's had enough to drink for the night. The water he had sitting out for her was perfect. After they were done eating, they walked into his room. She noticed his room consisted of a king-size bed and a flat-screen TV that was on the wall. He had one nightstand but no dresser. She looked in his closet and it was the biggest walk-in she had ever seen, with multiple drawers, shelves, and a huge space to hang his clothes. There were three full-length mirrors and a place to sit, in his closet. It was the size of her room at home. She was so jealous, and she told him that. He jokingly told her that she could have all the closet space she wanted in the spare bedroom that one was completely empty. She laughed and thought yeah right.

The music was still playing in the background, it was so soothing, yet erotic. Something about it made her feel sexy. The doctor looked at her and said, "Well, it's late, should we try to get some sleep?" He took off his towel and crawled into his bed, she took off her towel and crawled in after him, they were facing each other, and she smiled. She started touching his cock again, it was semi-hard and then she got it full-blown hard. She looked and him and said, "I guess now I know where you hide your surfboard," as she continued to stroke him. He looked at her and said, "You have quite the sexual appetite little one." She nodded and he started kissing her. She continued to stroke him, he kissed her passionately on her mouth and her neck, he whispered in her ear, "You want to ride my surfboard again do you?" She nodded. He ripped another condom off the strip and she said, "Surf's up!" in a frisky tone. He flipped her on her stomach, and he started kissing the back of her neck, her back, as he was caressing her body with his hands and kissing her, he kept moving down her body. She felt his mouth and tongue in between her legs. He started kissing and licking her wet flower. He told her how he loved tasting her and it didn't take long, and she gushed all over him. She was kind of embarrassed, it was more like an explosion. She thought for sure he must have taken special sex classes as a doctor; how did he know all her pressure points? He started to rub on her oh-so-wet flower with his fingers, he then positioned himself behind her, placing his cock in her vagina. He lifted her body up, leaned in, and whispered in her ear, "Are you ready to "Hang Ten?" he laughed playfully and lifted her in the air. He was standing on the floor and she was in the air, he was holding onto her by her waist as he kept pumping himself in and out of her. He wrapped his arms around her, holding her up against his body at times, kissing her neck and her back. He kept telling her how incredible she was. He thrusted into her, hard and fast. He let out a deep yell and then he thrusted into her one last time. He held her close, kissing her shoulders and neck, and then gently laid her down on the bed and slid out of her. He crawled into bed. She looked dazed. She had no clue how he did what he did, she looked at him and said, "You held me up in the air the whole time you fucked me like I was as light as a feather. I felt like I was flying like a bird." He laughed and said, "No, you were flying like an angel, towards the heavens, did you see the stars?" They both laughed. She kissed him.

They finally fell asleep. She woke up around 8:30 in his arms. He was spooning her. His body was so big it was like a blanket wrapped around her. She felt so safe with him. He felt her move, and he whispered in her ear, "Good morning sleeping angel." He said it in a sleepy voice, and he didn't move a muscle. That whisper stimulated her ear and the electric feeling went to every nerve in her body awaking her lady parts. Wow, the good doctor knew how to turn her on. She started rubbing her butt up against his body, she could feel his erection. She heard him rip off another condom. She liked hearing that sound. She could feel that he was putting it on, and she kept moving her body back and forth, rubbing up next to his, and then she felt it, he slid in her slowly. They both let out moans of desire. He moved in and out of her slowly and deeply. He was caressing her breasts with his one free hand and holding her close to his body with the other. He whispered in her ear that she drove him crazy. Her flower swelled. It started pulsating she was coming already. She said it out loud, "Baby, I'm coming all over you." She called him baby and that excited him. He whispered in her ear, I want to come with you, let me know when I get you there again. He started pumping a little deeper, and faster. She felt herself reaching her climax, and she screamed again with excitement, "Oh my God, I'm coming all over you baby." He thrusted into her and moaned loudly as he came.

She stayed at his place until close to noon. As promised, he drove her back to Oscar's so she could get her car. They exchanged numbers and agreed they should see each other again. She could not wait to see Keira and tell her about her night. She would not believe it.

Chapter 13

Dr. Heart texted Alex later that day asking when he could see her again. Her flower was sore, and she didn't trust herself being around him. She knew from then on, every time they decided to hang, they were going to be having sex. It was just too amazing to deny themselves. She responded to the text saying she could see him Sunday night if he was free. Sunday night worked for him. She drove to his place. And it was like Friday night all over again. Amazing sex, multiple times... But after their sexcapades, he desired to know more about her. He asked her about her family, and they talked about life in general. She shared with him about Darius. He was taken aback by her story. His eyes were tearful and sympathetic. He said, "That's why you cried?" He touched her face, wiped his fingers across her lips and looked into her eyes, and said, "I am so sorry you have had to endure such a loss."

She asked him why he was single. It didn't make sense. He was the complete package. He told her that he was in a serious relationship for 6 years while he was in residency and fellowship. His girlfriend wanted to get married but he wanted to wait until he was completely done with his fellowship. She ended up cheating on him with another fellow, who happened to be one of his closest friends in med school. They are married now. One of the reasons he wanted to move so far away. He was ready for a fresh start, new people, and new experiences. Alex looked up at him and could see he was still hurt by it. She didn't know what hurt more, the girlfriend or the friend betraying him. Either way, it sucked. Alex said, "What a stupid girl." He laughed and said they were both stupid and deserved each other. Alex laughed and then kissed him.

Over the next weeks and months, the doctor and Alex grew very close. They saw each other often. Not only did the doctor enjoy surfing he was also an avid cyclist. Alex loved riding bike too, so they spent a lot of time checking out different bike trails. The doctor would often stop by Alex's work when he was in the out-patient clinic, sometimes just to say hi quickly and other times they would grab lunch. Frequently, Alex would show up at work and there would be a note at her desk that said sweet things such as; *I can't wait to see you later* or *Have a beautiful day, Beautiful,* or *I can't stop thinking about you.* It would be signed with a little heart.

After two months, she decided to go on birth control, so they didn't have to worry about condoms all the time. He also gave her a key to his condo. She was staying there at least 4 to 5 times a week, and he wanted her to feel comfortable coming and going as she pleased. She loved the condo's work-out facility, it had the newest and best equipment, and the pool was amazing.

Chapter 14

The doctor had to leave for a two-day cardiology conference. He didn't want to leave Alex, so he invited her to join him. She had a lot of homework and thought while he was away, she could finish writing some papers. They texted and facetimed while he was away but Alex could not wait for him to come back home. She missed his company and the sex. He told her he would text her when his plane landed. Once she got the text, she knew she had about twenty minutes before he would arrive at his condo. She received the text and started feeling excited, yes, she even felt excited down there.

Alex got two glasses out and made two captain diets. She went into the bedroom and took off her clothes. She put on some over-the-knee high, black shiny boots, and threw on one of her favorite coats. It was a white fur coat with black stars all over it. She left the coat open. She took a few sips of the captain, and then she ended up pouring herself another. She was a little nervous to see him, it had been two days. She decided to play 'Drunk in Love' by Beyoncé, she loved that song and found it fitting seeing as Beyoncé sings about riding a surfboard in the second verse. The doctor walked into his home and saw her in nothing but the coat and boots. He smiled. The music was loud. She smiled at him but neither one of them said a word. She handed him the glass of captain, grabbed his other hand, and escorted him to his big, light grey couch. She motioned him to sit. He sat. She started dancing for him. As he watched her, he untied his tie and took it off, he unfastened the top three buttons of his shirt, he smiled a little boy smile and he continued to sip his captain. He looked sexually hungry. She could tell she was turning him on. She saw that he had to adjust how he was sitting. She kept dancing. She closed her eyes, she was feeling the music, she touched her body and then she looked at the doctor. He motioned her to come closer to him. She danced her way to him and then straddled him. She danced on his lap and he started unbuttoning and zipping his pants. He slipped his pants down and he placed his hands on her face and moved her face close to his. He kissed her. He told her she tasted like sugar. She smiled and licked her arm. She smiled and said she was wearing a flavored, shimmer body spray. She thought it tasted like vanilla icing, it was called 'Cupcake'. He smiled his sexy smile and he said, "MMMMM…. I like cupcakes." She was still dancing on his lap and smiled, "Uh, huh, you like sweet things….Did you miss me?" He kissed her again more deeply. Her flower was so wet, she wanted him bad. He looked deep in her eyes, with his lustful look, and said, "I missed you so much." It was like an electric current went through her body. She placed his cock inside her and she glided up and down on him. He stuck his face in her chest and started kissing and licking her breasts, he touched and caressed her. He licked any part of her body that he could get close to his mouth. He placed his hands on her ass guiding her on how fast and hard to go. She looked at him and her eyes did that roll-back thing that they do and he said, "You ready to come with me," she arched back and he lifted her up and moved her down slowly but pushed himself into her deeply, and then he went faster. They both screamed out as they climaxed. She kissed him and said, "I missed you too Baby."

Chapter 15

Months later the doctor told Alex he had to leave for a cardiology seminar. He was going to be gone for 4 days. He asked her if she would like to go since it would be the longest, they had ever gone without seeing each other since they met. He asked her many times before to go on works trips with him, but she always had a reason why she couldn't go. This time was no different. The morning he left for his trip, he kissed Alex passionately and told her he didn't think he could survive four days without her. As always, he would let her know once he was checked into his hotel and he would facetime when he had a chance. He kissed her again and then left. They facetimed or video chatted daily while he was away. On the second day of him being gone, Alex received flowers at the doctor's condo. They were sunflowers. They were so big and beautiful, and they happened to be her favorite flower. She knew he was in the middle of the conference when she sent a picture of her gratitude. She was naked on his bed with her legs opened. She had one sunflower covering her vagina to conceal it. She texted him saying, "My flower misses you and needs to be watered. Hurry home soon." She signed it with a flower emoji. They had amazing video sex that night. She loved knowing she could excite him even when he was miles and miles away.

Day four arrived, he would be coming home. She was a bit giddy. It had been four days since she had physically touched him, and she was missing his touch. She couldn't wait to see his face. He was going to be home closer to 6:00 so she decided to make dinner, a spaghetti bake. Pretty much the only thing she knew how to make well. She had a side of garlic cheese bread, a Greek salad, and strawberry cheesecake for dessert. She was wearing black laced booty shorts, and her 'The Used' black tank top that had a big, long dangly red heart on the front of it. She thought he would like the heart.

He texted her letting her know he was in the car and on his way home. She poured a glass of wine and started sipping. She had Levi's Bedroom Playlist playing in the background, and she was feeling good. He walked through the door. He was wearing a navy-blue suit, a light blue shirt, and a tie that Alex bought him. Their eyes locked. He ran up to her and picked her up. He kissed her deeply. When they let up for air, she said "Hi Baby", and he smiled and said "Hi" back to her. He told her he loved her little outfit and he traced the heart on her tank top with his finger. He looked at her and said, "Did you miss me?" she nodded her head. He put his arms around her and pulled her closer to him and he kissed her again. He said he was famished and whatever she was making smelt amazing. He took off his jacket and loosened his tie. He started looking around the kitchen to see what she was making for dinner. She looked at him and said no peeking. He laughed and then gave her a silver gift bag that had silver wrapping paper sticking out of it. "I found something I thought you might like," and he winked at her with a boyish grin. Every time he went away, he would bring her back some fancy panties or lingerie since he knew how much she liked "pretty panties" as she would call them. She loved his little gifts and was always excited to see what he picked out for her. She told him that dinner wouldn't be ready for 20 minutes or so. She suggested he pour a glass of wine and relax while she changes into her new gift, and she winked at him.

He poured a glass of wine and sat on the couch waiting for her to come out from the spare bedroom. Over the months she started keeping her stuff at his place, taking over the spare bedroom's walk-in closet. She walked out of the room. She was wearing a white laced teddy that was held together by one clasp in the middle. The clasp was made with Swarovski crystals. It looked expensive and elegant. It was the most beautiful piece she had ever worn. She ended up putting on high-heeled white booties to pair with the outfit. She walked towards him and stopped and turned around so he could get a good look at her. He leaned back on the couch and adjusted himself a little bit. He licked his lips and told her he was a lucky man. He looked at her booties and said he liked her heels. She smiled at him and said he could thank her mother for that. When she was a teenager she was told if she ever went to a boy's house, she needed to keep her shoes on because if she took her shoes off, other things could easily come off too. So, Alex would make it a point to keep her shoes on when she would have sex just to spite her mother. She smiled at him and started walking closer to her good doctor. He sat up a little and motioned her to come even closer. She did. He started touching her. He asked her again if she missed him. And she nodded her head. He then said "Really? How badly did you miss me? Show me." He started touching her lips and then gradually moving down to her breasts, and then down to her vagina. He snuck two of his fingers underneath the teddy and he felt her warm flower. He started playing with her clitoris. He loved watching her get all hot and bothered, for a while, she kept her eyes on his but she could only last so long. He knew how to pleasure her, and he knew all her erotic buttons. She started feeling that euphoric feeling that made her eyes roll back. Her nipples were hard, she was going to climax any moment, she was moaning, she started pulsating, she squirted all over him. When she was done, she looked down at him and climbed on his lap, straddling him. She started to kiss him. She was rocking back and forth on him. He was excited and oh so hard. He looked at her and took off his tie. He said, "I think you might have missed me. Don't you want to know if I missed you?" She laughed and said, "Did you miss me?" He grabbed her hands and tied them together with his tie, he slid her off his lap and laid her down on the couch. With his left hand, he held her hands up above her head, by his tie. He grabbed a sunflower that was in the vase on the side table, dragged it slowly down her body. He opened up her legs and then placed the sunflower over her crotch. He unsnapped the teddy, leaving her vagina exposed. He gently brushed the sunflower over her vagina, over and over it again. She started moaning, he asked her, "Do you want to know how much I missed you?" She nodded her head, saying yes. He then dropped the sunflower and put his face in her crotch. He started kissing her there. He licked her. He made love to her flower with his mouth. She was in pure ecstasy. She moaned and whined, she started moving violently, and then she exploded all over. He continued to kiss her there and then he looked up at her. He got up off of the couch, picked her up, and took her into the bedroom. He laid her down on the bed. He took his pants and shirt off. He took off his boxers and he placed himself inside her. Laying on top of her, kissing her passionately, he gently went in and out thrusting into her, and then he whispered in her ear, "I missed you so fucking much Alexandra." He fucked her hard and deep. They both moaned. She screamed that she was going to come, and he fucked her even harder and he let out a thunderous yell as he released.

Chapter 16

Weeks went by, it was about 9:00 PM on a Thursday night. The doctor was sitting on top of his island, eating cold cereal, watching the end of the Miami Dolphins vs. the New England Patriots game, wearing nothing but his grey Nike sweatpants. Alex walked into the kitchen and said she wanted a snack too. She laughed saying she was writing an exciting paper on business strategy and needed a break. She opened the refrigerator and went for a yogurt. The doctor casually mentioned that his father called him saying he was going to be in town for a conference the following day. He was having a business lunch early that day with colleagues but was wondering if he and Alex would give him the honor of having dinner with him later that evening. He thought D'Marcos would be nice?

D'Marcos was a new steak and Italian place in town. It was amazing, expensive but amazing. Alex loved the food there. She loved the ambiance. It was decorated old school, with pictures of the greatest of the greats all the Rat Pack, and the music they played was of course Frank Sinatra, Dean Martin, good ol' Sammy Davis Jr., Bing Crosby, Nat King Cole, etc... She loved it. Unfortunately, once again, Alex said she wouldn't be able to make it. The doctor was disappointed and wanted to know why not. She said she wasn't going to meet his family yet, that's not what their relationship was. The doctor looked at her and said, "What? What do you mean? What's our relationship? We aren't boyfriend and girlfriend? I'm sorry, YOU ARE MY GIRLFRIEND. We have been seeing each other for over 8 months, you basically live here. Mrs. Admondson, in condo 303 just gave us cookies the other day because she thought we were the cutest couple in the building. I'm not sleeping with anyone else, and I'm pretty sure you aren't either." Alex looked at him like she was in a stone-cold gaze, she snapped out of it like a light bulb went off, "Oh my God, you're right. I'm so sorry. I fucked up. This is not real. This is a fantasy. I have been so selfish. You don't even know me. I have been having fun with you, but this isn't real, you were just a distraction. We can't do this anymore. I can't do this with you anymore." He looked at her in panic, her words hurt him, "What? Ok, forget dinner with my father. Sorry if you feel pressured. He just wanted to meet the girl who has made me so happy these past months. There will be other times, you don't have to meet him tomorrow. But we are real, what we have is real, Alexandra. This is real. I know you. I know that when there is a song on that moves you, that you get up and dance, regardless of where you are. I know nothing brings you more joy than anonymously buying some random old couple's dinner when you see them out eating at a restaurant together, just because you like seeing old people still in love. Most importantly, I love the way you make me feel, you excite me, and I know I excite you." Alex interrupts him and says, "I think you are amazing. You literally are the best guy in the world, but you deserve better than me, more than me. You deserve to get married and have kids and be with someone like you." He jumped in, "That's not fair, who are you to tell me who and what I deserve? Someone like me? I don't even know what that means?" Alex started getting emotional, "You deserve all those things without baggage. I am damaged. Do you want to know why I am here all the time? Because I don't want to go home to an empty house. To live with the ghost of Darius. When I am here with you, I don't have to face the reality that he's gone and that's not fair to you." The doctor jumped in and said, "Then sell the house, move in with me." She darted a look of disgust and almost hate, "Sell my house? Like, forget he ever existed? Just move the fuck on???...FUCK YOU!" He had tears in his eyes and said, "No, he will always exist. He is a part of you. But you can love another person Alexandra. I know I cannot replace him. But you can love another person and I know you love me. And all I know is that I want YOU, YOU! I love you." With tears running down her face she said, "Baby, I don't want to hurt you." He jumped off the island and rushed towards her, he wiped her tears away and said, "Baby, baby, baby, then don't hurt me... don't leave me, Alexandra." He had tears in his eyes, he dropped to his knees and he hugged her body. She went down on her knees and kissed him. They made love on the kitchen floor.

The next morning the doctor left for work early. He kissed Alexandra goodbye and told her he would see her after he was done having dinner with his father. When he left, Alex packed up all her stuff from his condo and put it in her car. She left the key to his condo on the kitchen island. She walked out of his condo and went to work. After work, Alex went home, to her home. Around 9:30 PM she received a call from the doctor, but she didn't pick it up. He sent a text with the picture of the key and then a sad face emoji. She never responded.

The following Monday Alex went to work and there was an envelope at her desk with her name on it. She opened it up. The doctor's condo key was inside along with a note on an old prescription pad paper that read:

Alexandra,
You hold the key.
My heart is yours.
My home is yours.
I hope you find what you are looking for.

Dr. ❤

Chapter 17

Alex messaged Keira and asked her if they could meet at Oscar's. They decided to meet at 5:00 PM. Alex told Keira everything about what happened at the doctor's place, she also showed her the note that was left at her desk earlier that morning. She was teary-eyed but adamant that she should not see the doctor anymore. Keira was surprised because she thought Alex and the doctor might end up together. They seemed like the perfect match, but Keira understood that Alex was not ready to get into a serious relationship yet, and apparently, that was what the good doctor wanted. She felt like there was nothing else to be said. Alex needed her friend, and Keira was there. Keira spoke up and said, "Shots it is!" Keira ordered a round of patron shots.

When Jeff brought over the shots, Keira told him he could bring another round of shots with the tab, they had to leave in 15 minutes. Keira gave Alex her shot- and Keira cheersed her saying, "To feeling all the feels!" Alex smiled and winked at her friend as a teardrop fell from her eye. Alex nodded and they did their shot. Jeff came over with the 2nd round of shots and the tab. The girls paid up and looked at each other. Alex raised her shot and cheersed to Keira and said, "To good friends who are always the light in the darkness." Keira smiled and nodded as they did their shots. They got up from the table and walked outside. Alex walked Keira to her car and gave her a big hug. She thanked Keira for coming out and said it was just what she needed.

Chapter 18

Keira was happy that Jess, Sadie, and Alex were all there now. She couldn't wait any longer and looked directly at Alex, "Did you ever get a response from the priest?" Alex looked at Keira and said, "No, I am sure he is still praying about it." She sounded down but chuckled, "You know I am the Delilah to his Sampson." Of course, she had to nickname their little whatever it was after characters in the bible. It was outlandish to think that a priest and a sex toy lady like Alex, would have such a deep connection and relationship, but they did.

Two months ago, Alex saw on Facebook that her priest's parish was destroyed by an earthquake. There was a GoFundMe page created to help repair the damages to the church. Alex donated money anonymously. She knew how much the church meant to the priest; she was just so relieved he was alive and safe. She watched him on live feed whenever he posted on Facebook. Anything to see his face, hear his voice. The last message she sent him was on Facebook. She could see that the message was opened but he never responded. She wasn't surprised, just disappointed. She knew the bishop would advise him to resist temptation and her sweet priest belonged to the diocese. He made a promise of obedience to the local bishop and a promise of celibacy. Alex thought it was complete bullshit and was irritated that her priest signed up for that. What a waste. Why did he feel the need to sacrifice so much of himself, and for what? It's like he felt like he needed to be punished or something.

It was now December, a week before Christmas. She sent him another message on Facebook. The message was just checking in on him, hoping he was safe and doing well. She did however sneak in there that she thinks of him often. Alex did not believe in lying or pretending her feelings away. Life was too damn short, and she wanted her priest to know how she felt, surely it was alright to let him know she thinks of him, right? She also wished him a Merry Christmas, a bright, adventurous, safe and prosperous New Year. She meant every word. She never received a response. It was only two days, but still, if she hadn't heard from him by now, she wasn't going to, maybe never. That really bothered Alex. Keira was the only one that knew how Alex felt about the priest, and she could see the anguish in Alex's face.

Alex admitted that maybe getting rejected by the priest might have bruised her ego, but that aside she was just disappointed in him. She felt he was never going to stand on his own, never going to think for himself. He switched from being a member of the judicial system to a member of a religious organization. Both dictate what you should believe, what you should think, what is right and wrong, and it was bullshit. There is no one person or group of people that should be allowed to play God. Yes, there should be some authority to keep peace and give guidance, but there is no way everything is going to be black and white. In the judicial system, people are wrongly convicted daily because a judge or group of one's peers decides another person's fate. Religious organizations are a crock. Besides all the bat shit crazy molestation and cover-ups that have been publicized, it's the religious views and judgments that bothered Alex the most. How can one human being be appointed to be judge, jury, and executioner of someone's soul?

Not only was she hurt that she never heard back from the priest, but she was hurt because he was following orders from someone else and not making his own decisions. She thought he was being brainwashed and frightened that he would never have a real, true, fulfilling life because he is not allowing himself the gift that God himself gave us ALL, and that was the freedom of choice.

Chapter 19

The Priest

Alex was a clinical assistant. Her job was to document all the clinical information for the doctor before the doctor came in to see the patient. Her first patient of the day was a few years older than her. She wasn't used to seeing people around her age at the clinic. Usually, they were way older, so she was looking forward to having a younger patient. She escorted him back to the examining room to ask him the standard questions. Alex was pleasantly surprised he was actually very good-looking. He was about 6'1, thin with a runner's build. He had short, brown hair, light brown eyes, and he was dressed professionally, wearing slacks and a navy-blue sweater. He was very polite, charming, and had this calmness about him. They started chatting about the weather, and his trip there, seeing as he was from out of town. They discussed the reason for him being at the clinic. He was there for low back pain, she thought to herself, *that must dampen the sex life; I can give him some pointers.*

Normally, the clinical workup takes 15 minutes or so but Alex knew the doctor was going to be late, so she took her time and visited with the patient for 45 minutes. Within that time, she learned that he was there for a 2nd opinion on his back, he was a stressed-out lawyer from New Orleans, and he was single. He mentioned he was in the process of switching occupations. He was planning on joining a seminary close by, actually only two hours away from where Alex lived. Alex thought he had a great presence about him. He was very calm, gentle, witty and he was easy to talk to. She could see him being a great pastor but a priest? Doesn't that mean no sex? EVER? It was none of her business, so she obviously didn't ask, but she thought it was a shame.

He ended up staying a couple of days for some additional appointments. He had a follow-up visit in Alex's area to get treatment recommendations. Alex was happy to see his name on the schedule again. She went out to get him from the lobby and when she called his name he looked up from his chair and he looked right at her. They both smiled. He had a twinkle in his eye, and it melted Alex's heart. They went back to the examining room and they discussed that it was his last appointment and he was looking forward to hearing about treatment options and ready to going home. He was not a huge fan of getting poked and prodded. Alex sympathized.

He mentioned that he was flying out the next day and was looking for things to do to kill time. He liked to hike and asked her if there were any great trails around. Alex knew of some decent ones close by, she also liked hiking. Without really thinking about it, she asked him if he would like to go hiking with her the next day; it would be a Saturday, she didn't have to work and had no solid plans. He smiled and said he would like that a lot, way better than going on his own and he liked visiting with her. She gave him her number and told him to call her Saturday morning if he still felt up for it. There was a great nature center that had some amazing trails and the scenery was beautiful. The priest called her the next morning around 8:30 and wanted to know if she still wanted to go hiking. Alex thought 10:30 would be a great time to go so she offered to pick him up at his hotel at 10:15. His hotel was 10 minutes away from her house. Alex was happy he called. She was excited to see him outside the clinic and she was looking forward to the hike. She was a bit nervous about what to wear. She wanted to look cute, comfortable, for sure cute but at the same time, it's not like anything could come of what they were doing. She was just being friendly and he was going to be a priest for God's sake, she should not care what she looks like. Even though she did find him very attractive, she needed to keep that out of her thoughts. She put on some jeans, a t-shirt and threw on a zip-up sweater, that she could easily take off if she got too hot during the hike, and she wore hiking tennis shoes. She packed some snacks, water bottles, and a couple of thin blankets just in case they found a nice place to sit and visit for a bit.

The priest was waiting outside his hotel for Alex. She drove to the front of the hotel and as soon as she saw him, her heart started racing. She could not believe she was doing this. He was seriously a stranger and she only knew him from the visits that she had with him in the clinic. But for some reason she was not scared, she was excited and felt drawn to him. If anything, he should be scared of her. He didn't know her either, and he was going to hop in her car, she could take him anywhere, dump him anywhere. Alex thought he looked delicious. He was wearing sunglasses, dark blue jeans, a white t-shirt, and a brown and cream plaid flannel, untucked. She was happy she asked him to go hiking with her- she loved this look on him, the relaxed look, and seeing him outside the clinic. When she pulled up to the front of the hotel, she rolled down her windows and said, "Hey You! You ready for an adventure?" He smiled big and said, "Hey YOU!" He opened the door, got in, looked at her, and smiled. Alex said it seemed like time froze as they just stared at each other, smiling, and then she started to drive. She was very attracted to him, and just being in his presence gave her this warm feeling all over. She couldn't explain it. She just liked being around him. She kept telling herself, don't think more into this than it really is, this is just a fun afternoon. He is going to be gone and you will never see him again.

The nature center did not disappoint. They hiked for two hours and then they came upon an old cemetery. It was ironic because it was a resting place for nuns and priests that passed on centuries ago. Alex thought it was the perfect time to lay out the blankets and chill for a bit. They talked a lot about him working at a law firm in New Orleans. Alex could only imagine how stressful it would be to be a lawyer, but she was also confused as to why he would switch from being a lawyer to a priest. It just seemed bizarre to her. He said he just wanted to help people. He was raised by his mother. His father was killed in a car accident by a drunk driver when he was five years old, leaving him, his mom, and his little sister. They struggled to make ends meet. His mother worked two jobs for a while just to pay the bills and put food on the table. The Catholic Church in their neighborhood ended up offering his mother a job as a secretary. She was able to quit her other two jobs and spend more time with him and his sister. The church always made sure that their family was provided for. When he was a little boy, he promised his mom that he would grow up and help those less fortunate. He wanted to do everything in his power to make sure he did things that helped feed the poor, take care of the sick, and that there was accessible, good, and affordable housing for all.

He was hoping he could help people less fortunate as a lawyer but instead he found himself defending murderers, robbers, and thieves. He was finding loopholes and legal technicalities that got his clients out of the trouble they were in. He saw how crooked the judicial system could be and he didn't want to be a part of it anymore. He hated knowing he allowed really bad people out on the street; people who have and will potentially harm other people.

What he was saying made sense but why did he have to become a priest? It bothered the living shit out of her. He seemed like a cool, regular guy. He was obviously very compassionate, and he had a heart for people. But she couldn't picture him being a priest. She thought priests as being stiff and as of lately, the media publicized that a crap-ton of dioceses across the country were under investigation for priests molesting boys. So, she had to ask him, "Are you going to be a priest, like wear a chastity belt, no sex, priest?" He nodded his head. He explained that he felt like becoming a priest was truly his calling. He had been running from it for so long but now he knows that's what he should be doing. As a kid, the only safe place for him and his family was the church and he felt like he needed to give back and dedicate his life back to the Catholic church. He acknowledged that it might sound crazy, but celibacy is one of the biggest acts of self-sacrifice. Celibacy is known to be a special gift of God, which allows the priests to follow the example of Christ more closely. Christ was pure and he wanted to be more like Christ. He went on to say that when a priest announces his service of God, the church becomes his highest calling. If he had a wife or a family, there could be a huge possibility for conflict between his spiritual and familial responsibilities. He said the Vatican considered it easier for unmarried men to commit to the church because they would have more time for devotion and fewer distractions.

Alex had a very upset face, and he laughed and asked her why it was bothering her so much. That was the wrong question, because once he asked, she let it all out, all her thoughts on religion and how she thought it was a crock. "Have you looked in the mirror? Good Lord. You are frecking hot baby. What a waste. Do you honestly think God wants you or anyone to make such a sacrifice? Man is the one who made these rules of the Catholic church, not God. Do you think making such a sacrifice will clear your heart and mind of any romantic or sexual desires? You are human, you are naturally going to have those desires."

She went on to explain that men and women of the church hide behind religion to control people. She shared with him that her parents were prevalent church members and missionaries. They often preached about God's love and forgiveness. Yet, her parents were in a loveless marriage and she told the priest that her mom beat her relentlessly as a kid. "Look at all the priests in the news for child molestation. Do you think they would be raping kids if they were allowed to have sex? They vowed never to get married, but hey, it's ok if they fondle a kid or stick their dick in a kid's face. What the heck??? History will repeat itself, and there will be a huge cover-up and no one will have to own up for their sins - this shit has been going on forever. Who is protecting the kids? I just find it ironic that these people speak of God's love while they abuse kids! That's not God's love. And these so-called people of the cloth have the audacity to tell others what is right or wrong? And to ask you to stay single so you don't get distracted and only focus on the church. What a crock!"

Alex went on to say, "The rules of the church are a joke. Relying on a bishop to tell you what is right and what is wrong, all the while you have priests out there fucking little altar boys. When will they wake up and realize that denying one's sexual instincts and desires does more harm than good? You not having sex for the rest of your life does not benefit you or anyone else. God does not care if you have sex. He actually wants you to have sex. He created you to have sex." Oh, she was fired up. He seemed to be taken off guard. She was very passionate about it. She went on to say, "Do you know that sex increases your blood flow triggered by a surge in nitric oxide in your body during sex? Sex boosts your immune system, and when you reach an orgasm, oxytocin gets released and dopamine increases. Oxytocin is known to wipe out cortisol, the major stress hormone. When you have an orgasm you actually release serotonin and dehydroepiandrosterone (DHEA) at climax. Serotonin regulates mood and makes you feel happy and relaxed. DHEA has antidepressant effects and it boosts your immunity. These are all good things. Maybe you need more sex and less church? UGGGG...Ok, Ok...fine be a minister, a pastor, a missionary, but a priest? Lock it up and throw away the key? WHY?? It's ridiculous!"

Then Alex realized she totally flew off the handle, she didn't know this guy at all really. Why does she give a flying fuck if he never gets to have sex with another human being? Not her problem and she's never going to see him again. He was just looking at her, he started laughing and then she started laughing. As he was sitting on the blanket, he took off his sunglasses and looked at Alex, it seemed like he was trying to choose his next words wisely. Alex sat down closer to him and she looked into his eyes, they looked sad in a way. Alex thought to herself, *I would have sad eyes too if I signed up not to have sex with another human being for the rest of my life.* It was such shit. She touched his face. It was so soft. He closed his eyes as she moved her finger down his face and across his lips. He opened up his eyes and he leaned in closer to her as if he was going to kiss her. She looked at him and said, "I guess it's not like you can't release all these great hormones yourself, just sucks that you won't be able to experience such ecstasy with another person. That human connection when a man and woman become one is amazing." He nodded and sheepishly said, "Well pleasing myself is another thing I would have to refrain from. That would be giving in to my flesh." He looked down at his feet and couldn't look up at Alex. He then explained that he had sex before it wasn't like he was a virgin. He said he had many girlfriends in his past and a serious girlfriend while he was in law school. He didn't get into too much detail he just said it didn't work out. He said it was just another sign he was on the wrong path. Alex thought maybe he had a broken heart and that's why he could swear off sex forever. Alex could understand that. Keira kind of did the same thing. But to never touch himself again, WHAT THE FUCK?!

It was getting late and he needed to get back to his hotel, pack up and head to the airport. When they got to the hotel, he asked her if she wanted to come in and visit while he was getting his stuff together. Without hesitating she said sure for some reason she felt entranced by him and she didn't want him to go. They went to his hotel room and he finished packing. He had about 30 minutes before he had to leave. They both were sitting on the bed. Alex apologized for getting so heated at the cemetery. He laughed and said, "Yeah, what was that about?" She looked into his sad eyes again. She leaned in and kissed him. She felt the need to be closer to him, he reciprocated. His kiss back was intense, passionate, and incredible. She was stunned. He was so good at it. He cupped her face in his hands, and looked deep into her eyes, he touched her lips with his fingertips, she bit her bottom lip gently, and he went in for another deep kiss, she was awestruck. She could feel her flower swell and get wet. She could tell her eyes were dilating, she called them her bedroom eyes. She whined. He continued to kiss her and then they laid down on the bed. They continued to kiss. He was holding her. He told her she was beautiful, and that he wished he met her earlier in his life. There was something about her, he felt good being with her. It was natural like they have known each other for years. Alex shared she felt the same way. She felt calmness and peace when she was with him. She had no cares in the world, and she was excited by him. They continued to kiss. Alex yearned for more but knew she shouldn't even try. She needed to be respectful. She cared enough about him not to be selfish. She thought to herself just be happy he kissed you back without feeling the need to say five Hail Marys afterward.

Time was up and he had to go. Alex didn't understand why she felt the way she did, she didn't want him to go. She thought they had this crazy connection and didn't want to lose that, it felt important. They had each other's numbers and became Facebook friends. He was going to reach out to her when he moved to the seminary, maybe they could reconnect. They texted back and forth; and talked many nights on the phone and when he moved to the parish, he let her know where he was. She looked it up, it was an hour and sixteen-minute drive from Alex's home.

Chapter 20

Alex and the priest continued to have friendly conversations multiple times a week. They talked a lot about heaven and hell. Alex was curious about the subject and wanted to know his thoughts on where a person goes after they die. She wanted to know if he knew for a fact if there was a heaven. She also wanted to know his thoughts on God's love and his forgiveness. He revealed that when he was in law school, he got his girlfriend pregnant. She did not want the baby. She had two years left of law school. She worked hard to be where she was at and didn't want to risk everything to have a child, not then. The priest was willing to make the sacrifice, but she was not. She had an abortion. It wrecked him. He said he struggled a lot with his girlfriend getting the abortion, he was completely against abortion. They broke up six months later. She wanted to move on and forget it ever happened. He could not. After a while, he couldn't face her, and he said it wasn't her, it was the fact that he put her in that situation. She had every right to do what she wanted with her body, but he wished he could have saved his own child, fought for his child. He called himself a sinner. He said he ran from God for so many years, being self-involved, and yet here he was at his lowest low, finding himself running back to God, begging for forgiveness. He asked for guidance and for God to heal his heart. He said he felt an overwhelming sense of peace wash over him. The priest knew his child was with God. He went on to say that God forgave all of us of our sins, he is no respecter of persons, he does not show partiality. He shared that God's love was the best kind of love, it was unconditional. He said, "When we are in pain and hurting, God is also in pain and hurting with us. He suffers and triumphs with us. He is always with us. We are never alone, Alexandra." He believed that to be true. When he talked about abortion, everything clicked. That must be why he is willing to make such a huge sacrifice.

She trusted the priest. He shared things with her that she knew he didn't share with anyone else, and she knew she could share anything with him, and he would not judge her. They had a very deep connection and she knew if he could handle her freak out at the cemetery, he would be able to handle anything she threw at him. They talked about regular things too, like her family, her work, school, and her dreams. He talked a lot about his sister and his mother. He shared with her all the things he was learning in the seminary. He traveled a lot. They visited other parishes, and they also ventured out into the community and he really liked those days. He went all over, he traveled to Guatemala, Rome, Italy, Amsterdam, and Israel. He talked in detail about his healing experience while swimming in the Dead Sea. He was even learning Spanish. It sounded amazing. And for the most part, he sounded happy and excited about what he was doing.

She loved hearing about his adventures, but she wished she could be with him. Alex wasn't allowed to visit him. The rules of the parish were extremely strict and if they saw each other, it would be as if they were sneaking around. She would be considered a distraction and he was supposed to be devoted solely to the church. He didn't want to mess up. She was disappointed but understood. She was secretly hoping he would try the priesthood thing for a while and realize it wasn't for him and then maybe they would be able to reconnect for real. No holds barred.

Chapter 21

One night the priest called Alex just to check in like he often did. Alex told him she couldn't stand him calling her anymore. She didn't even know what they were doing. It was teasing her. She felt like she was his dirty little secret. They were friends secretly by phone and Facebook. She felt like they had a secret relationship, and he was her secret boyfriend. They talked about everything. She knew things about him no one else did. They confided in each other and it was obvious that they had romantic feelings for each other. They even joked about what their life would and could be like together if he didn't go into the priesthood. Would they get married and have kids, they decided on anywhere from 4-6 kids, or just travel the world and see what they see. They both loved adventures and wanted to experience other cultures and different parts of the world. With every phone call, she was reminded that he would never be allowed to be in a romantic relationship, but for her, she felt like they were already in one without the sex. No one knew her like the priest. She felt vulnerable and scared that one day he would be taken away from her altogether. How would she handle that? She didn't even know what the point was with him contacting her, she couldn't even see him in the flesh. She had to stalk him on Facebook just to see his face, just to see where he was, and see what is was looking at. She wanted to share those experiences with him. With each phone call, she felt rejected by him with just the reminder that they were not allowed to be more than friends. She felt dirty and not good enough, and it brought back all the memories of her growing up. Putting trust in her family and religion but left rejected and judged. He apologized to her and said it was never his intention to hurt her or cause her any pain. She was not a secret, and he would never think of her as dirty and he never wanted to hear her say that again. The more he tried to comfort her the more agony she was in. She wanted to be with him. She wanted to feel him, touch him, she wanted him. She told him that. She asked him, "Don't you want to touch me, feel me, be with me?" He was quiet and then he admitted "Yes, I do… but I can't allow myself to think or talk that way. They're impure thoughts. I'm going to be taking the vow of celibacy soon, we can never be more than what we are."

Alex wanted to know why the thoughts were so impure. Natural thoughts that a man should be allowed to have towards a woman he cares about, why is that impure, and who is the one that makes these rulings and stipulations? She thought it was all unfair and wrong. They weren't her rules and she refused to live by them. She wanted to be where he was. She wanted to be with him, physically. She wanted him to touch her, she missed his touch. She told the priest she was imagining him there with her, touching her, and kissing her. She wanted to know what he was wearing. He said he was wearing a button-up shirt and jeans. She told him to take them off and be with her. She needed to experience something with him. Her flower was throbbing for his touch and she started touching herself. The priest told her he shouldn't be having this conversation. She begged him to stay on the phone with her. So he did. She could hear him breathing. He said her name softly. Alex started moaning, she loved hearing him say her name. Every time he whispered it, stimulating shock waves went from her inner ear all the way down to her lady parts. The thought of him made her excited, but the sound of his voice took her to a whole other level. She told the priest she was touching his face, she was kissing him and she moaned while telling him how she loved the way he kissed her and touched her, she hungered for more of him, she begged for him to say her name again, and he whispered "Alexandra," he repeated it again and again. She moaned "Yes, yes don't stop," She described in great detail every move she was making, she said she was unbuttoning her white shirt, letting her breasts free and she wanted him to touch them, kiss them. She described the little red and black plaid mini skirt she was wearing and told him she wasn't wearing any panties. She wanted him inside her. She needed to feel him. She said she was going to sit on his lap.

She wanted him to continue to touch and kiss her. She asked him if he loved touching her and if he wanted more of her. In a breathless voice, he said, "Yes, yes I want you, Alexandra." She told him how she loved making love to him. He felt incredible. He called out her name again, with a deep sound of desire, she could hear him breathing heavily, she told him not to stop touching her, she needed him. He said, "I won't stop" he whispered her name, she moaned that she was coming. He kept whispering her name as he moaned.

After Alex regained her composure the priest apologized and said they couldn't do that anymore, they can't. He wants her too, but he needed to pursue the priesthood. He acknowledged that they were struggling with their friendship and maybe he shouldn't call as often, if at all. He said it was his fault, he never meant to cause her any heartache. He cared for her deeply, but he was feeling torn between the priesthood and being with her. He wanted to comfort her, but he was concerned that them staying in touch was torturing both of them, and he didn't feel like that was right either. He never knew anyone like Alex. He was extremely attracted to her. She spoke her mind and wasn't afraid. He admired her fearlessness and her passion. They had a connection that was undeniable. She captured his heart and he didn't know what to do about that. What he felt for her was true and he wanted her to know that. He was not teasing her but he needed to seek council. She told him he needed to do what he feels he needs to do, not what someone else thinks he should do. She wanted to know what he wanted. She yelled, "If you want me, I'm here, so close you can reach out and grab me; yet, you are going to ask someone else what you want? What you should do? What you should have? Reach out and grab me! I am here!!" He told her he needed time. Alex hung up.

Chapter 22

Weeks and months went by. Alex would get random text messages from the priest but no phone calls. The text messages were letting her know where he was on his travels, finding new trails she should visit, and when he saw something she would like, he would send her a picture. Sometimes she responded, sometimes she did not.

The priest sent her a song through Facebook messenger by Taking Back Sunday, one of Alex's favorite bands, the song was '*My Blue Heaven*'. The song is a love story that talks about the lives of a guy and girl that collide together, they get involved in each other's lives in some form or another. The guy is tortured with heartache over the girl. He wants to tell her how he feels and just wants to give in to his feelings. He knows it's a bad situation and all his feelings keep getting stacked up inside of him, making all the pain and agony he feels inside worse, even though he is going through so much torment swaying between what he knows he should do and what he wants to do, he cannot deny her in any way, whether it's having feelings for her or physically being with her. There's a verse where the singer refers to the guy as a patient boy and a jealous man at the same time, he's waiting and longing to be with her but at the same time he knows she is with other guys, finally, he gets the balls to tell her how he feels. The guy begs for her to listen to him, give him a chance and return the same feelings, he wants it more than anything and he admits, "Sometimes it just feels better to give in," and at the end of the song he bellows out, "It's you I can't deny," and the story is left unfinished.

Alex knew the song well and it resonated with her and the situation she had with the priest. Hearing the song and knowing he sent it to her did not help with the heartache. She now knew he was being tortured as much as she was. The pain was real but there was nothing she could do about it. He made his decision and she didn't know what he wanted from her.

More months went by, she got a phone call from the priest. He had a challenging day and a weak moment. He was telling Alex how tormented he was. He couldn't stop thinking about her. He wanted her, and he told her all the things he wanted to do to her. He shared deep, dark sexual desires with her. He began telling Alex that he wanted her to touch him. He needed her as badly as she needed him. She instantly got warm in-between her legs. Hearing him whisper his desires made her body tingle, his words excited her. She wanted him too. But her conscience got the best of her and she told him to hold on, to slow down. She had to ask more questions. She wanted to know what was going on with the priest school. Was that still something he felt called to do? He said he was confused. She felt so guilty. She could tell he was torn between his passion to serve the church and his passion to have a hot romance with her. She was sick to her stomach. She didn't want him to quit if he wasn't sure, and she wasn't going to convince him to quit and leave everything to be with her, because she knew she couldn't commit to a relationship. She was a mess. She had playboys she was messing around with and felt the need, to be honest with him. He made it clear months ago that he wanted to pursue the priesthood and they could not be more than what they were. It wasn't like she was sitting at home watching Hallmark movies, waiting for the phone to ring and him to say he was ready to jump ship and come be with her. She actually didn't bet on that at all. Alex told the priest that she was hanging out with other people, she was having sex with guys. What did he expect? She admitted that she was still a mess and would not be able to promise him anything. Did he think she would be like, "Oh my secret boyfriend decided he NOW *thinks* he wants to be with me?" What if it's a weak moment and he changes his mind again. She couldn't stand being toyed with. She would love a chance to be with him, but she couldn't say jump ship and let's run away together. She didn't know what he wanted from her. He was taken aback by her honesty and confessions and most likely, hurt. He apologized saying he didn't expect her to wait for him and knew that wasn't fair. She apologized and said she never wanted to be the reason why he would quit his journey to the priesthood. She would never want him to resent her. She wanted it to be a decision that he made solely on his own. The apologies didn't matter, the damage was done, and the words were said. He realized he made a mistake. He confessed he shouldn't have called. He shouldn't have expressed his desires and longings for her. It was a weak moment. He hung up the phone abruptly. Alex was hoping she would get another phone call like that again, and perhaps she would give him a different answer. But that was the last phone conversation she had with the priest.

Chapter 23

Every once in a while the priest would message Alex letting her know he was at the same baseball game she was at. He saw her posts on Facebook. The priest's parish would often go to the Twins baseball games in the summer and he knew Alex went to the games a lot too. He would always message her after the game to let her know he was there too. It killed her. Why did he wait until after the game? Time passed and Alex was experiencing a drunk, vulnerable moment. She called the priest, he didn't answer so she left him a message sharing her thoughts with him. She laughed and said, "Since you're a priest, abiding by the rules and all, the least you could do is take my fucking confession." She only thought it was fair. She told him she wanted to be with him. She needed to feel him. To touch his face, to kiss him and hold him. "Why can't you give me what I want?", she shouted in frustration. They didn't have to have sex, she just needed to be with him. She needed to be in his presence. She didn't understand why it was so wrong for them just to see each other. She was pissed at him. Later, she sent him a text message telling him she was pissed that he made the decision to be a priest. It didn't make sense to her. He was denying himself any chance of having a romantic relationship with anyone. She knew him and knew he loved children, he would make a great husband and an excellent father. He deserved those things if he wanted them, and not necessarily with Alex, but anyone, she knew he deserved to fall in love, be loved, feel loved, and have all those things. Who was Alex kidding? She wanted him. She would have been crazy jealous if he ever ended up with anyone other than her. She didn't care what the consequences were, she needed to tell him. She texted him, "I want to see you. I need to see you. This is killing me. You're killing me." He never responded to the text. The next morning, she wondered if he was going to block her. But he didn't.

Chapter 24

Time went by and the Priest messaged Alex through Facebook letting her know he was moving to a different parish, back to his hometown in Alaska. She looked it up, it would be over a six-hour flight or a fifty-six-hour drive. He then went on to tell her that he genuinely wished her much happiness. He thought she was a unique and "unrepeatable" person. He said he would always continue to pray that she finds true and deep happiness. The message made her sick to her stomach. She found it cold and robotic. He was moving on, he was leaving her, and he was telling her she should move on too. She never heard from him again. She would Facebook stalk him and watch any live feeds he would air for his congregation. Alex would watch just so she could see his face and hear his voice. He looked exactly the same; still handsome, with the same sweet and kind demeanor. Sometimes his face was clean-shaven but sometimes he had a beard. She liked the beard. It was short, clean-cut, and framed his face perfectly. She watched the live feed and would take snapshots of the priest. She would blow up his face so she could look at his sweet face, his eyes, his oh so sad eyes. Yes, they were still so sad. She left him Facebook messages letting him know that she was stalking him, was it wrong, she didn't know what else to do. She couldn't get him out of her head. He wasn't talking to her so all she could do was message him, she texted him saying she couldn't leave him alone, she vowed she would keep an eye on him until the day she died, she needed him in her life even if it was virtual. Just because they weren't talking didn't mean she didn't miss him, and she was hoping the feelings were mutual. She felt so sick, obsessed, and twisted up in the head, but she needed to tell him, who else could she tell? She wanted to know why God let them meet if they could never be together? What was the point to all of it and why was she so drawn to him? It was a different kind of agony. She thought it might be similar to the agony Keira felt when she found out about her husband. The betrayal, him still being alive, living a whole other life without her. Her loving him and not being able to actually love him. How did Keira deal with it? She prayed for indifference. Alex thought that's what she needed to feel towards the Priest, indifference. Otherwise, she would never get past the obsession.

When she heard about the earthquake that destroyed his church, she tried reaching out to him, but no answer. She messaged him to wish him a Merry Christmas, no answer. She could see on the live feed that he was alive and safe. She was at least comforted by that, however; she was saddened knowing she wouldn't be hearing from him ever again. He probably knew if he responded, the vicious cycle of heartache and torture would continue. Alex would jump at the chance to take the road-trip to see him. She just wanted to see him, touch him. She would give anything just to be in his presence again. Alex felt like the leper in Leviticus 5:3 of the Bible. The leper broke social conventions and the law in desperate attempts to get help. Back in the Bible days, it was against the law for anyone with skin diseases to touch others, but the leper believed if he just touched Jesus he would be healed. He was determined to see Jesus, touch him, despite the crowd and his disease, he came before Jesus and touched him, knowing he was unclean, and it was forbidden, BUT he was instantly healed. Jesus embraced the leper without hesitation. Alex felt unclean, and forbidden to see her Priest, she had a strong desire to reach him and to touch him. She wished he would embrace her without hesitation. She laughed to herself and thought, *well, the Priest did want to be more like Christ.*

Chapter 25

Jess looked at Alex not fully understanding why Alex was so bothered by not hearing back from a priest and says, "So the priest has conformed to a bunch of bullshit, that's his choice, Alex. He made his choice. He could always leave but he hasn't. Maybe he is happy? Seriously, his loss Girl. And while we are talking about happiness, what's going on with Pretty Boy? Oh, my goodness girl – keep him for as long as you can. I still can't stop thinking about that time we went to see him with Church." Alex laughed, "Yeah that was a fun night."

Pretty Boy

Alex made the decision to go back to college to finish her bachelor's degree in business. She only had five classes left. She was going to take one class at a time, it was going to take her a little over a year, but she didn't have anything else to do. When Alex started her fourth class she met this one, good-looking, cocky kid in her class. It was her first and only class with him. He looked like a model. He was gorgeous. Every time she looked at him all she could think of was, "Man, he sure has a pretty mouth". Every time he talked – the words that came out of his mouth were annoying, but she pictured herself, biting, and licking his mouth, or even better, sitting on his face. She wanted to taste him in the worst way. He was young, 21-years young. He was tall, 6'1, skinny, but athletic. He had dark skin, dark eyes, and dark hair. Alex thought he resembled a younger, Jason Momoa, the guy who played Aquaman. Hello deliciousness all in a package, and what a package he had. Yes, Alex hit that. She hit that a few times. No one in the class had a clue, and it was defiantly their little secret. Their college was a Franciscan college, so their casual, sexual liaisons would have been frowned upon.

Chapter 26

Alex's business management teacher was a young hip lady. Alex really enjoyed being in her class because the lectures were relatable and kept her attention, unlike most of her other classes. The fun thing about this teacher was she wanted the students to learn outside the classroom too and Alex loved getting out of the classroom. The teacher said she wanted the class to break up into partners, find a local business of their choice and do a short presentation on business. She did not want it to be a big box store or chain, like a Target or Applebees, she was thinking more along the lines of the local watch doctor, or the family-owned ice cream parlor down the street. She wanted the students to interview the business owners to find out what they thought their key to success was. She wanted it to be fun and encouraged the students to pick something they were interested in. They had five weeks to identify a business, interview the owners and present their findings. She also told the class she knew that they usually pair off on their own, picking their own groups and partners but she wanted to shake things up a bit and decided to randomly assign partners. As luck would have it Pretty Boy and Alex got paired up.

When Alex heard Pretty Boy's name and her name together as partners, she instantly felt flushed. All she kept thinking is, 'Oh great! How am I going to be able to work with this kid? All I think about is sitting on his pretty face.' She looked up at Pretty Boy. He was smiling at her. Alex nodded and smiled back at him. She instantly got butterflies in her stomach. The teacher allowed the partners to get together during class time to exchange ideas and contact information and make plans on how they would accomplish everything. They had about an hour before they would be dismissed. The teacher reminded them that the presentation was due in five weeks.

Alex walked over to Pretty Boy to say hi and figure out what they were going to do. This being their very first time actually speaking, it was a bit awkward and uncomfortable for Alex. She asked him if he had any ideas on a local business. He mentioned there was a dance studio that was downtown that they could possibly check out. Otherwise, he had some friends that worked at a bar that was kind of like a club, and maybe his friends could help get an interview with the owner. Alex loved that idea. Pretty Boy said the only thing was the club was not just locally owned. The people who owned it lived up in the Twin Cities and had clubs up in the cities too, so they decided the club might have been considered a chain and no longer an option. He asked Alex what she was into and if she had any thoughts. She embarrassedly smiled and said, "Well, it might be inappropriate for our school, but I was thinking we could interview the owner of Sexy Fun and Sexy Secrets, the adult stores. I know the owner personally, and I am sure it would be nothing to set up a meeting with her. Sexy Fun is actually like a party store for adults and Sexy Secrets is her lingerie store." She smiled innocently and said, "That was my only idea. But the dance studio would be awesome too. What do you think?" Pretty Boy smiled and laughed saying, "Oh we are going with the sexy stores." Alex smiled and nodded her head and said she would make the arrangements.

They decided to meet on the weekend to work on their presentation since Alex worked day shifts during the week, and Pretty Boy worked mostly nights during the week and weekends. Alex made plans for them to meet with the owner of Sexy Fun and Sexy Secrets that upcoming Saturday at 11:00 AM. the owner's name was Susan, Alex called her Sexy Susan. Susan was definitely sexy. She was a very tall blonde, that had long flowy hair. Alex thought they had to be extensions because her hair was so full and healthy-looking. Susan had a great body, and a great rack, Alex assumed she had a lot of plastic surgery done, she looked like barbie. Sexy Susan always looked and smelt like a million dollars; she dressed nicely; her nails were always manicured to perfection. She had the appearance of the ideal boss lady. Alex admired her.

When Alex and Pretty Boy walked into Susan's office, Susan smiled and welcomed them with a very Sexy Susan embrace. She hugged Alex first and then she looked at Pretty Boy, and said, "OOOO... Alex, you have been holding out on me. I need someone this delicious working for me." She touched Pretty Boy's arm, and felt his bicep, she smiled a lustful, sexy smile and laughed and said, "Welcome. So nice to meet you. Any friend of Alex's is a friend of mine. Please excuse me for being so excited. Alex told me that you two are interviewing me for a class project? I love projects". She giggled.

Pretty Boy explained that they wanted to know about her business, and they were hoping that they would be able to identify what Susan thought her key to success was. Susan smiled and said, "I am an open book." Susan shared that she inherited the Adult Store from her uncle. She said it was the typical adult store, people had the idea that the adult store was a store that sold sex. You could read about sex, watch movies about sex, and experience sex. When her uncle owned it, the customers were older, blue-collar men. Some young men came in, but typically the age range was 40-65. She, like everyone else, had misperceived ideas about her uncle and his store. She thought of her uncle as a pervert, she was frightened to walk in the store, assuming it would be filthy, with come covered, sticky floors, and maybe even a backroom where guys were jacking off, and possibly strippers or prostitutes accompanying them. She laughed, and said, "Yeah, I have quite the imagination". She went on to say as she got older and more mature, she realized that her uncle wasn't a pervert at all. His store was clean, in the cleanliness sense, there were no guys in the backroom jerking off, and no prostitutes or stripers anywhere to be found, and most importantly the floors weren't sticky. She admired her uncle because he saw a need and he had the balls to open up a store to fulfill those needs, regardless of the social norms. His business was okay, he didn't make it rich, but he lived comfortably, and he liked what he was doing. When Susan was of age she started working for her uncle at the Adult Store.

Susan said she and her uncle became close and ended up becoming partners. She gave him great ideas to facelift the store, to give it more of a welcoming and fresh appearance. She added more items to the store besides magazines, books, videos, and toys, she added lingerie, lotions, and oils to enhance the sexual experience. She convinced her uncle that they should try to appeal to a larger group of people, not just middle-aged, blue-collar gentlemen. They could try to attract a younger crowd and women too. She voiced that she wanted to do a romance display for Valentine's day. She created romantic baskets filled with a variety of oils, lotions, and couple sex toys inside. She also placed pretty, laced lingerie on racks beside the Valentine's basket display. The regular customers thought it was kind of cool, some of them bought the baskets for their wives or girlfriends and paired it with a piece of lingerie. Her uncle was amazed at how popular the baskets were. He had customers coming in asking for them, and not only men, women too.

As her uncle aged, he decided to give the store completely over to Susan. Susan changed the store's name to Sexy Fun. She had just a little sign on the door that said 18 and older only, not one of those big neon signs that said "ADULT ONLY" she thought those signs were cheesy. Understanding that some people were still afraid of the stigma behind walking into an adult store, and being looked at as a pervert, Susan expanded her business to also provide her items online. She also hired a few ladies to provide at-home parties to introduce new products and allow people to buy directly from the ladies, in the comfort of their own home, instead of being caught walking in the store. She smiled and winked at Alex, and then said, "Ladies like Alex, she is one of our best party ladies". Alex smiled and blushed.

Susan explained that as the business grew, she decided that she needed a second store. She really wanted a high-end lingerie store, but she thought it best to have that store be located closer to retail stores on the north side of town, appealing to women and men who like to shop in the higher retail stores. She named the store Sexy Secrets. Sexy Secrets sold high-end lingerie, bras and panties, spa items such as bubble bath and bath beads, and massage oils and lotions. She kept Sexy Fun on the south side of town, near all the bars and restaurants. Sexy Fun was more geared towards bachelor and bachelorette parties, birthday, and romantic parties. It had more novelty-type items such as the penis and boob straws and suckers, blow-up dolls, adult toys, lubricants, oils and lotions, role-playing costumes, lingerie, and platform heels and boots.

Susan conveyed that she believed the key to her store's success, besides keeping it clean and inviting, was knowing who her customers were, what they wanted, staying along the lines of supplying a need. She also said being willing to change and keep up with the times by paying attention to the trends was important. She mentioned that she recently added pole and belly dancing classes to a list of things she is getting involved with. Fitness is a new trend in the community and to captivate some of the fitness expeditionists', she's started offering pole and belly dancing classes on Thursday nights and Saturday mornings. The dance studio was in the basement of Sexy Fun, and she had a professional come in and lead the classes. She kept the classes small and spots filled up quickly. She might be offering more classes if the demand keeps up. Lastly, she said, "Location is very important, you want to make sure that wherever you put your business, it fits nicely with the businesses around it, creating great traffic flow into your store. Many people might walk into the store, not knowing it was there, but just because they happened to be next door shopping, they might wander into your store and check it out".

Alex and Pretty Boy spent an hour at Sexy Fun. Susan walked them around the store and showed off some hot merchandise that she can't keep on the shelves. Pretty Boy admitted he had never been in an adult store before. Susan gave him a goodie bag full of samples and told him she hopes after this visit, he will become a regular customer. She winked at him and gave him and Alex hugs goodbye.

Chapter 27

Alex and Pretty Boy met a few times on the weekend to work on their presentation. Alex was surprised and a bit impressed with how intelligent the kid actually was. On the surface, he seemed like a cocky prick, but he was actually pretty smart and normal one-on-one. Alex found out that he played baseball in high school and was offered a full scholarship to play for UCLA. Unfortunately, he hurt his right shoulder playing his senior year of high school, and the injury cost him the scholarship.

He also told Alex that his parents were both doctors and were hoping he would go into the medical field, but he really wanted to go into a business geared towards fitness. He wanted to create and own a work-out facility that catered to professional athletes. He shared with Alex his dream of having a high-end, state-of-the-art, work-out facility that had the best training equipment and studios with trained instructors, and physical and occupational therapists on site. He also wanted it to include summer camps for younger athletes who wanted to perfect and enhance their performance. It was going to cost a lot of money, so he would need investors if it was ever going to work. He knew he needed to create a kick-ass business plan, and he was hoping he would learn something from these classes that could help him. He really wanted to network with fitness groups and he was hoping with the help of his parents, he would connect with people in the medical field that could help add input to his proposal and get on board with his dream.

Chapter 28

One night after working on their presentation, Pretty Boy asked Alex if she wanted to grab some drinks. She thought why not. They ended up going to a bar on the north side of town that he frequented a lot. He had some buddies that worked at the bar. They seemed happy to see Pretty Boy walk in. They gave Alex and Pretty Boy drinks on the house. There was hip hop music playing, a DJ booth, and a huge dance floor. There were high-top tables and chairs all around the dance floor and wall to wall huge flat-screen TVs playing different hip hop music videos. Pretty Boy saw Alex looking around … and he said, "Yeah, isn't this place insane? This is the club I told you about when we were trying to decide on a business to interview. This place is different than the average dance club. The dance space is not just for dancing, it's for competitions, like dance-off competitions." He seemed very excited to show the place off to Alex.

Alex and Pretty Boy had a couple of drinks and visited for a bit about different music genres, dance techniques, and culture. He talked about how he liked to learn about all kinds of dance, not just hip hop but he liked ballroom dancing, swing, jazz, and even ballet. He liked how music and dance was a way for a person to express themselves. He said he worked out a lot of his emotions through music and dance, especially after he hurt his shoulder. He thought of dance and music as healing therapy. He said it saved his spirit. Alex was shocked. He was passionate about it and Alex thought that made him even more attractive. She could relate to a lot of what he was saying.

A hip-hop mixed song came on and Pretty Boy jumped up and looked at the bartender. The bartender changed the lights, nodded at the DJ, and the music volume went up. Pretty Boy went out on the dance floor and he started dancing. He had some crazy, intricate freestyle moves. After about 30 seconds, someone joined him on the dance floor and challenged him. The battle was like something Alex only saw in the movies. She was so impressed with Pretty Boy's skills. When the battle was over, the dancers did some hand slap, and then Pretty Boy walked up to Alex, grabbed his drink, and slammed it. He was all sweaty but super sexy. He ran his hands through his hair breathless and looked at Alex and smiled. Alex was staring at him in awe and with excitement said, "Holy crap dude, that was AWESOME!" He said, "Thanks, but watching an actual dance-off competition is better, usually it consists of dance teams that have practiced for months. They show up and bring everything they got. The choreography is always mind-blowing. If you liked what I did, you'll have to come back when they are doing competitions. Honestly, it's ridiculous how talented some of these cats are."

The more Pretty Boy talked the more intrigued Alex was by him. After a few more drinks Pretty Boy took Alex by the hand and took her out to the dance floor. Alex felt like an idiot dancing with him because he was so good at it. He did some break-dancing hip-hopping moves that amazed her. He tried teaching her a few moves. They shared lots of laughs because Alex was not very graceful, she was pretty sure she looked foolish, but she was having fun. Alex noticed it was getting close to midnight and she thought she better get home. She had to work at 7:00 and then they had class later that night, so she needed to get some rest. She thanked Pretty Boy for bringing her out to the club. She had a great time and said she would definitely come back to check out one of the dance competitions. He smiled at her and said, "I'm actually cool with leaving now too." He waved bye to the bartenders, grabbed Alex's hand, and walked out the doors with her. She thought it was odd that he grabbed her hand. They walked out and she started walking towards her car. He was still holding onto her hand, he rotated his arm to spin her around in a circle. She giggled. He pulled her in closer to him. She saw his face, his mouth, he was so beautiful. He smiled and he kissed her. Just a soft peck on the lips. His lips were big and soft, "I had a blast tonight, Shorty. You're fun." She laughed. He smiled and bent down kissing her again, this time he opened his mouth and slid his tongue in hers. It was a sensual kiss. She started to think what the heck is going on here? Pretty Boy made a cute face and said, "Do you really want to go home? Or do you want to go to my place? I have captain." He winked. She laughed. "Sure, you had me at captain. I will follow you in my car."

Chapter 29

Pretty Boy lived about three blocks away from the bar. She followed him into his place. Alex was pretty buzzed and not really sure if it was a good idea for her to go there. He walked in the kitchen and put on some Post Malone while he made a couple of captains. Alex said, "OOOO...I like a little Posty." He laughed and looked at her t-shirt, "I figured." She was wearing a Post Malone tank. Alex looked down and laughed. He handed her the captain and told her that he has lived in the townhomes for about a year. She thought it was an odd comment but nodded her head and said she thought they were nice. Quickly she was thinking she made a huge mistake coming to his house, was this a friendly nightcap, or was he trying to fuck her? Or maybe he was a serial killer? She looked at him and said, "I am sorry, but you are fucking hot, what are you doing here with me?" He laughed and said, "You're fucking hot too. What do you want us to be doing here?" She looked up at him and jumped up in his arms like a koala bear and started kissing him. She wanted to devour him. He laughed and said "Ok, whatever you want, Shorty. All you had to do was ask." He kissed her and carried her into his bedroom. He kept her in his arms and showed her his room and said, "Alex, Bedroom, Bedroom, Alex" he gently let her down on his bed. He took off his white t-shirt. He had a full sleeve of tattoos on his left arm. He was buff, she could see he had a 6-pack and he had a tattoo on his right side but she couldn't make out what it was. He took off his jeans. He was wearing bright red boxers, and he slid them off too. Holy shit, the kid was packing. He knew he was living large. He had a shit-eating grin on his face. Alex took off her shirt and slid out of her short shorts and threw them quickly to the ground. She was wearing a yellow lace bra and matching panties. Pretty Boy smiled and said, "Hello Yellow." She laughed. He crawled on the bed and went to kiss her. He lifted up the blankets and slid underneath them, grabbing Alex's hand, she followed. He leaned over and moved her hair out of her face and kissed her. He said, "You taste like candy, even your hair tastes like candy." He laughed and said, "Kind of like sweet tarts." Alex kept kissing him and said, "Good, that's what I was going for, it's actually called Candy. It's an edible body spray." She laughed and continued to kiss him. She was happy she kept that body spray in her car and remembered to refresh herself with it, especially since they had been out dancing. She was relieved he was tasting and smelling candy instead of tasting salt and smelling onions. He briefly stopped kissing her and said, "You know the samples I got from Susan, I know what to do with the oils and lotions, but I don't know what this is for." He leaned over and gave Alex a little jar. It was the nipple tingler. Alex explained that he could put it on his nipples and or his partner's nipples and it starts to tingle when warm or cool air goes across it. She explained that it was great for partners who like to play with nipples, when they kiss or lick the nipples it tastes good plus the recipient, gets that tingling sensation, and it's a turn-on. She told him it was a win-win. She said it also works great if women like the look of hard nipping out nipples, you rub that on, and the nipples get hard and stay erect for a long time. He laughed. She said, "Here, let's put it on your nipples and mine, you can feel what it feels like and then taste what it tastes like". She unclasped her bra. She put some of the tingler on his nipples and then she put some of it on her nipples. Pretty Boy kissed her lips and then kissed her neck and then he went to her breasts giving her nipples a lot of attention. Alex moaned. Alex pushed him back and started licking his nipples and he laughed and said, "Holy shit." Alex said, "Yeah, cool, right? Erotic feeling and strangely the tingler works great as a lip balm too. This is a good flavor too, raspberry, yumm!" Then Pretty Boy kissed Alex's lips. He began to kiss her neck and then up to her ear. She started kissing his shoulder, his chest, arms, and any part of his body that got close to her mouth. He laughed and said, "My whole mouth is tingly and my nipples are so sensitive right now." He scooped her closer to him as their bodies rubbed up against each other. They continued to kiss and rub up against each other. She was wet and he was wet too. Before she had a chance to ask, he grabbed a condom from the shelf by his bed and he put it on. He pulled down her panties. They continued to kiss, they were laying sideways, facing each other, and he slid his cock inside her. His eyes rolled back, "Damn" is all he said. He slowly pushed himself into her, he went in deep, he moaned every time he would pull back and then thrust back into her. He started going faster and then he moaned loudly. He came. Alex did not. It could have been because she had too much to drink, or just because it was her first time with him, or maybe it was because she was too damn busy watching him in awe. She loved watching his face as he climaxed, and she loved feeling him press into her when he came. He looked at her intently and said, "Holy shit. You're AWESOME!" She really didn't do anything, she was just there, he did most of the work. He kissed her a few more times and then slid out of her and then got up out of the bed. He took off the condom and went to the bathroom. He came back with a warm washcloth. He gently wiped her vagina with it. She didn't say anything. She didn't know what to say. She just wondered who taught him to wipe someone's flower after sex, that's unique, and she liked it. It was warm and it cleaned out all the condom and wet juice stuff. He went down on his knees by the bed and pulled her closer to him. She was laying on her back, and her legs were dangling off the bed. He started kissing her leg and then the inside of her thigh. He kept kissing her, going up closer to her flower, and he looked up at her and said, "Don't worry Shorty, I'm gonna take care of you." He spread her legs open and went straight to her flower. She could not believe this fucking gorgeous kid was kissing her there. She had fantasized about this very moment over a hundred times. He knew what he was doing, she started moaning, moaning louder, seconds went by and she got warm, her eyes rolled back and she started having convulsions. He held on. She climaxed and came all over his pretty face. He made sure he got all the juices she squirted out. He continued kissing her down there and then moving to her right inner thigh and her left inner thigh, then he began kissing back down to her feet. Alex was numb. When he was done, he went back to the bathroom rinsed the washcloth with warm water again, and wiped her flower again. He crawled into bed and curled up next to her and whispered, "What music do you like to listen to when you are going to bed?" Alex said, "Cigarettes After Sex." She laughed a little bit. He changed the music to Cigarettes After Sex, and then he turned her on her side and spooned her. He kissed her on her neck, her shoulder, and her back and whispered, "Sweet dreams." He fell asleep.

After about 30 minutes, Alex got out of bed. Got dressed and left his house. She jumped in her car and thought *What the fuck!* she had no idea that was going to be her night. It was now 2:30 AM. She thought maybe she could still get 3 ½ hours of sleep if she crashed right away.

Chapter 30

Alex made it through work, she had just enough time to grab some food before class. She was a little bit nervous because the night before was crazy, and she was hoping Pretty Boy wasn't going to act weird after what they did together. Alex decided to go to the pub across the street from the school and grab a burger and beer before class. Pretty Boy texted her, "Hey Shorty! Sorry I didn't get a chance to say bye this morning. I guess you wore me out. I'm looking forward to seeing you in class and doing our presentation." He added the emoji smiley face with hearts going around its head. Alex responded with a smiley face and texted, "I'm at O'Neil's across from the school, grabbing food and a beer before class. Liquid courage!" Pretty Boy texted back, "Do you want some company?". Alex texted, "YES! That would be awesome. I'm belly up at the bar." Pretty Boy responded, "I'll be there in 10." With a smiley face and two beers emojis.

Pretty Boy showed up at the bar, he ordered a burger and a beer. He looked at Alex, smiled, and said, "So last night was fun. I re-played the whole night in my head, multiple times, all day long." He laughed. "I wanted to text you as soon as I woke up but didn't want to freak you out. I hope you don't think I'm a dick?" Alex totally did not think he was a dick. She actually felt bad about misjudging him. He seemed sensitive and nice. She laughed, "Oh Baby, don't think twice about it. Last night was fun and spontaneous, but I'm not expecting anything from you. It is what it is. No worries." She smiled, and he nodded his head. He said, "I've never met anyone like you, most girls" he paused and looked at her sheepishly, "my age are annoying. Lots of drama. You're just cool. You're open and you're hot! Like I want you to meet my mom." He laughed. Alex laughed and said, "Let's not get crazy. Girls your age can be a little over the top. But if you haven't noticed, you are the hottest guy in this bar, on this street, and most likely in this town" Alex laughed,

"Maybe in the whole U.S. It's got to freak girls out. Young girls are insecure, and when they are insecure, they act crazy. Believe me, I know, I used to be young." Alex laughed again and then said, "Don't worry, the right one will come along, and she'll like and want all the same things you like and want, it will all just click. And she won't be crazy, she'll be cool like you. It might just take a few tries. You're so young, Oh God, you're so young." Pretty Boy looked at her and kissed her passionately, and then said, "See, right there, you are so fucking cool; Can I keep you?" They both laughed. Alex said, "Let's just get through this class."

It was time for Alex and Pretty Boy to do their presentation. They had a lot of fun with it. Pretty Boy brought the samples to class with him and allowed the classmates to try the flavored lotions and oils on their arms. He also brought a sample of some strawberry nipple tingler. He instructed everyone to put it on their lips. It was smooth and tasted sweet like strawberry. He warned them that it would give off a tingly sensation so as not to be alarmed. He explained that it could be used for other things besides lip balm, he told them it was created to be placed on the nipples. It was a great item for couples during foreplay, especially for women and men who like attention in those areas. Everyone in class loved the presentation, there were tons of questions and the teacher was impressed with how well Alex and Pretty Boy worked together. They had amazing chemistry, they collected all the necessary information and then some, she appreciated them having fun during the presentation and at the same time keeping it informative and professional.

Chapter 31

Alex was pretty sure Pretty Boy was a male whore, he was too gorgeous and too smooth not to be, and she didn't care. He was just way too pretty not to get around. Alex could not keep her mouth shut about Pretty Boy. She had to tell the girls at happy hour that following week. He was hot as fuck and she had many nights of fun with him. Just his looks alone caused her panties to gush.

Pretty Boy was not a bartender but a waiter at a local Italian restaurant. He texted Alex inviting her to come see him at work. Alex wasn't going to go alone so she invited anyone willing to go. Jess and Churchie, were the only ones able to make it, seeing as it was a Thursday night, and everyone else had to work early the next morning. Pretty Boy made sure the girls sat in his section. They ordered appetizers, a few bottles of wine, and a few bonus bottles of wine. Churchie, born Rachael Churchill, her friends called her Church or Churchie for short, was in rare form. She hadn't been out in a while; it only took half a drink for her to warm up to Pretty Boy. Churchie was usually quiet at first but after she warmed up, there was no filter, and her friends loved her for it.

Churchie had short, strawberry blonde hair. She spiked it. She always wore crazy, fun dresses, and high heels, the higher and chunkier the better. She was single, and never had a boyfriend. She traveled a lot for work and always dreamed that she would meet a man while she was traveling abroad. She claimed she never wanted kids, she had two cats at home and for her, that was enough responsibility. After her first full glass of wine, she let Pretty Boy know how pretty he was. When he asked if they wanted to order any dessert, Churchie said only if he was on the menu. She told him he was the chocolate mousse cake, and that she knew what to do with mousse. Pretty Boy winked at her and said, "I bet you do princess." And the girls all busted out laughing.

Alex liked that Pretty Boy knew how to handle himself and how to deal
with women, especially older women hitting on him. He didn't seem
shocked or disgusted by it, he played along, and he was fun.

Churchie then started telling Alex about all the things she would do
to a man that was as pretty as Pretty Boy. Alex was getting embarrassed,
but Churchie didn't stop. Churchie leaned in closer to the table. She
started slapping the top of the table with her hand, spanking it,
screaming, "What's your daddy say? What's your daddy say?" Her
boobs were about to spill out of her dress. At that moment Alex and
Jess decided they better pay up and get Churchie the heck out of there.
They made it out of the Italian restaurant probably minutes before they
were going to be asked to leave. Churchie ended up cashing out for the
night. She took a cab home and promised Alex that she would text her
once she made it home safely. Jess and Alex were not quite ready to call
it a night. They wanted to go to another bar. They heard there was live
music playing at a local bar downtown. It was only a couple of blocks
away, so they started walking there. Alex and Jess loved live music and
they both loved dancing. Alex started getting text messages from Pretty
Boy asking if she was going to stop by his place later. She responded
saying maybe in an hour or so. He texted back that he would leave the
front door unlocked. He knew Alex was a night owl, and if the bar was
playing live music, she would be on the dance floor. He also knew it
could be closer to bar close before she would make it over to his place.

Jess and Alex were a lot alike. They liked the nightlife, talking to
strangers, listening to good music, dancing if the mood was right, and
forgetting about all the-day-to-day bullshit. Jess worried about her
family a lot. Shortly after she moved here, she found out her mom was
having a lot of health problems. She went home as much as she could to
see her family and help her dad out on the farm, but the distance was a
bitch. Jess felt guilty about leaving home but knew it was the right move
for her, nonetheless, she still felt guilty and missed them terribly.

Alex finally heard from Churchie. She texted that she was home safe.
She said she had a great night but was pissed she didn't ask for some
chocolate mousse cake to go. Jess and Alex laughed. It was late, the bar

was closing, and Jess needed to get home. She had to work in 6 hours. Her apartment was only 8 blocks away, so she walked home. Alex was not done for the night. She headed over to Pretty Boy's.

Pretty Boy lived in a two-story townhome. She started walking up to his townhouse thanking God she had a few drinks in her. She needed the liquid courage to be with this kid. He was young, but oh so hot. It was definitely just a plaything and they both knew it- no way that was ever going to get twisted. She walked up to the door and checked it to see if it was truly unlocked, and it was. She walked in and saw he had some candles lit in the living room, there was some music playing in the background, it sounded like Latin sexy sex music. She walked down the hall, and there was a door slightly open at the end of the hall. She walked into the room and saw Pretty Boy lying on the bed, face down. His bedroom was pretty bare, basically just a bed and a TV. He had rope lights on in his room, some candles lit, and she could hear the music just loud enough to hear it but not be overwhelmed by it. He was completely out. Pretty Boy always had the best music. He introduced her to all kinds of music, which was one of her favorite things about him. For a young guy, he was well diverse in music, and his dance moves were unbelievable. He could breakdance, freestyle dance, ballroom dance, you name it. He put her to shame.

Alex took everything off but her black, laced, cheeky panties, and climbed into bed right up next to him. She started rubbing his back, she loved his back tattoos. He had the words ROYAL across the back of his shoulder blades and he had a sign on his lower back – in the tramp stamp spot, it was the symbol for the Greek god, Hermes. She started licking and kissing his back. Sensually kissing and licking his tattoos. He let out a little moan, that made her flower wet and swell a little. As she continued to kiss his back, she kept thinking, God this kid is gorgeous. He rolled over, facing her, and said, "Hey Shorty." She saw that pretty mouth of his. She had to kiss it, lick it. She even gently bit his bottom lip. He kissed her back. He was such a sensual kisser. He rolled on his back; and placed her on top of him. He was wearing black basketball shorts. She could feel his member underneath. He was raring to go. She

didn't know what it was about skinny, tall guys, but damn, the good
lord must have thought that the "Johnson" was the right place to give
them all the girth because this kid had it. Alex said she liked the music
and wanted to know what they were listening to. He told her it was
Havana Nights. She nodded her head. Alex noticed there was a piece of
chocolate mousse cake in a plastic to-go container on the shelf next to
his bed. She reached over for the container, and Pretty Boy said with
a sexy smile, "I overheard something about chocolate mousse." Oh, he
was cute. Alex opened it up and wiped her finger across the top of the
cake. She slid her mousse-covered finger in her mouth to taste test it.
It was sweet and fluffy. She went back for more but this time instead
of putting the mousse in her mouth, she smeared it generously on her
nipples. Pretty Boy knew that was his cue, he started licking and tickling
her nipples with his tongue and then he started kissing multiple parts
of her body, anything that was within range of his beautiful mouth.
He grabbed her breasts. He was so eager to please. Alex moaned with
desire as she rubbed her body up and down his. She could feel his hard
cock underneath his shorts, she loved sliding up and down... it felt so
good. She was getting so wet. She went back for some more mousse,
and this time she wanted to put it in his mouth, so she did, and then
she kissed him. God, she loved that mouth. He then spanked her little
ass and said, "You know what daddy likes" she laughed and gave him a
sexy look and then kissed him passionately. They made out for a while
exploring each other's bodies, using the chocolate mousse any chance
they could. Finally, Pretty Boy had enough of the foreplay, he reached
over to the shelf by his bed and pulled out a condom. They changed
positions multiple times, Alex counted it, she had three orgasms and
thanked God for this pretty boy she was laying next to. What a beautiful
creature he had created and his work was good. She laughed. Her mom
would be so proud of her for taking the time to thank God for all His
wondrous works and her blessings.

4:00 AM rolled around and Pretty Boy wanted to play Rock Band
on his Xbox. Alex watched him for a bit but needed to get home and
shower before work. She worked up a sweat and the mousse left her a

bit sticky. She was tired and was hoping to get a quick 30-minute nap in before work, but it wasn't going to happen. She didn't care. The night out with the girls and with Pretty Boy was worth it. She told Pretty Boy she had to bolt, he stopped his game. He looked at her and said with a pouty face, "Ok Shorty, see you later?" She didn't like committing to anything so she told him that she would text him once she knew what the rest of her week looked like. He seemed bummed but took that answer. He then said, "There's an extra chocolate mousse cake in the fridge for your spiky-haired friend." And he winked at Alex. Alex ran over to him and kissed him. Ooo.. he was good. She kissed him on his lips, and then she went on to kissing his neck, and up to his ear. He had a big diamond piercing in his ear, Alex liked to kiss it with her tongue, knowing it drove him crazy. She whispered in his ear, "Good play Pretty Boy, good play." She liked a guy that took care of her and her friends. It showed he paid attention, she liked that. She went to the fridge and grabbed the cake, walked towards the door, and looked at his pretty face again. He smiled, and she blew him a kiss goodbye. He pressed play on his game as she walked out the door.

Keira loved hearing Jess's version of Pretty Boy; it only confirmed all the stories Alex told her about him. He sounded delicious and was bummed she hadn't seen him in person like Jess and Church were able to. Keira hadn't heard much about him over the past few months so she assumed since Alex and he were no longer in class together, they must not be hanging out as much. It was probably a little out of sight out of mind sort of thing.

Chapter 32

Sadie asked, "Have you seen Peter Pan recently or are things still weird?" Alex answered saying she hadn't seen much of him since their Florida trip. Keira loved hearing about Alex's adventures with Peter Pan, they always did something fun. That's how he got the nickname Peter Pan, he was the boy that would never grow up. He was 29 years old and lived in a duplex. He had a broken-down car, that only worked half the time. He didn't seem to care though because he lived right downtown, close to work and close to all the bars and nightlife, plus Alex had a car, so if they wanted to go anywhere that required them to drive, they would just take her car. Alex was a bit annoyed by a lot of that, maybe she was jealous that he had such a carefree attitude. Since she was a teen, she worked hard to save money and be independent. She started working at age 14, sometimes having multiple jobs. She saved up all the money she could so she could move out of her parent's house as soon as she graduated. When she moved out, she was in an apartment for a year and realized how much money she was wasting on rent. It irritated her so much that she worked her ass off to make sure she could buy her first house by the time she was 20-years-old.

Alex enjoyed all the fun she had with Peter Pan, but it was all just fun. Peter Pan liked sports, he loved to travel, and he liked Alex, and he enjoyed all three at the same time. They would travel to watch sporting events, or take day trips to lay on the beach somewhere; they even went up to Peter Pan's family's cabin for a weekend. They went on one big trip together to Florida. It was an interesting venture and most likely would be their last one together.

Peter Pan

Peter Pan worked in the finance department at the hospital Alex worked
at. He was 6 feet tall, with an athletic build. He wore his hair short
and it was so dark it was almost black. He had amazing bright blue
eyes. Alex met Peter Pan at a softball tournament that he was in with
a group of her friends. After the tournament, the players all went out
for pizza and beers to celebrate getting 2nd place. Alex was invited to
come with them since Jess was on the softball team and wanted Alex to
join them. The group ended up staying and playing pool and darts. They
split up in teams, and as luck would have it, Alex and Peter Pan ended
up on the same team. Alex found Peter Pan attractive, nice and funny.
He was kind of a clown but a bit on the preppy side. Alex could tell he
knew he was a good-looking guy, he was flirtatious, but he lacked some
confidence. Alex couldn't put her finger on it. There was a girl that was
hanging on him a lot. Alex assumed it was his girlfriend but later found
out she was actually his sister. His sister teased him a lot in a flirtatious
way and called him by the nickname Stacey. Apparently, when he was
born, his sister wanted a baby sister, not a brother, so she decided to call
him Stacey instead of calling him by his actual name. I guess her family
thought it was cute and allowed her to continue to call him that because
29 years later, she's still calling him Stacey. Alex was a bit confused and
the more the sister drank, the more annoyed Alex was by his sister.

While playing darts, Peter Pan and Alex talked about their jobs and
she found out that he worked in the business office for the hospital. His
degree was in communication, he played lacrosse in college and he used
to teach little league baseball. He said he really enjoyed teaching the
kids and said he would have loved to have done it as an occupation, but
it didn't pay. He didn't like his finance job, but he liked the money and
the benefits. His sister jumped in and told him that she was bored and
wanted to go home. He looked at her and nodded. He finished his beer
and told Alex he played darts every Wednesday night if she wanted to
join a dart league, they were looking for people. He encouraged her to

send him an email at work. He smiled, and his sister grabbed his arm and they walked out the bar.

Chapter 33

Weeks went by and Alex had an insurance question that came up at work, so she decided to email Peter Pan for help. After he helped her, they continued to email back a fourth. They enjoyed the conversations so much that they decided to meet up for a couple of drinks. They met at a local comedy club that was in between both of their workplaces. Alex found out that Peter Pan was originally from the cities, and he moved to town for a girl. She was a single mom with two kids. He dated her for about a year but eventually broke up. He said he stayed with her way longer than he should have, but he really liked the kids. Unfortunately, he hasn't seen the kids much after the break-up because she was crazy. He said he thought about the kids a lot, but he just couldn't be stuck in the drama. He decided to stay in town because of his job and the friends that he met. Alex enjoyed hanging out with Peter Pan. It was very casual. She felt comfortable with him, he was good-looking, and she thought it wouldn't be such a bad idea to hang out with him again. She thought about joining his dart league or at least subbing a couple of times if they needed a person. It was an option. He didn't seem like the type that would get hung up on her. He loved hanging out with different groups of people and he was pretty chill, not really a committed bone in his body, more like a fly by the seat of your pants kind of person. She liked it. From that point on they continued to see each other on a regular basis as drinking buddies.

Chapter 34

Alex spent a lot of time hanging out with Peter Pan and his friends at baseball games, hockey games, and sports bars. Alex kind of thought of herself as one of Peter Pan's wingmen. She got along great with his guy friends, and sometimes there were chics around too, hanging on the guys, some even flirted and hung on Peter Pan. Peter Pan was cool with it but a lot of times he would just talk to Alex. It didn't bother her because she really just liked hanging out with Peter Pan. She found him attractive of course but she really just enjoyed being friends with him and his friends, and that's all she really needed from that relationship. She made it crystal clear that she was not planning on ever getting married again or falling in love.

Peter Pan and Alex had a blast hanging out doing anything and everything that came up. Peter Pan was more into sports but he knew that Alex was more into music and live bands, so they went to a few concerts together. Peter Pan's sister lived about two hours away from Peter Pan, so when she wasn't in town visiting him, she would constantly call or text him. Peter Pan and his sister did a lot of things together on the weekends. His sister was a few years older than him. Alex understood having a close relationship with a sibling and having an older, protective sibling, so maybe that was all it was. It was still kind of odd. Alex also realized that his sister could be feeling left out because now that Alex is hanging around, maybe he is not spending as much time with his sister as he used to, believe it or not. Alex was trying to give the sister the benefit of the doubt, obviously, she was important to Peter Pan, so she needed to keep her thoughts to herself about his sister.

One- night after dart league, Peter Pan asked Alex to come to his place for a late-night, nightcap. She thought, *why not?* They went to his place. It was cute actually. He made it very homey. It was a two-bedroom apartment. He converted one of the bedrooms into an office space. The kitchen, living room, and bathroom were all decent sizes and he had them decorated in sports themes. She also noticed a ton of pictures of Peter Pan with his sister all over the house and Alex thought that was a little wacky. It made her think of the Friends episode when Rachael was dating a guy that had an unusually close relationship with his sister and Rachel catches them taking a bath together. Yeah, Alex thought for sure that this could be a very similar situation. Alex said something to Peter Pan about the pictures of him and his sister. He laughed and admitted they were very close. Alex smiled, but thought, *NO SHIT!!!*

He mentioned his sister helped him paint the walls in the living room, it was a buttercream yellow. Alex thought it was nice, but she was more of a cappuccino girl when it came to painting walls. His house was very clean and neat. Peter Pan offered Alex a white Russian, that was his drink of choice right before bed. Alex gladly took it and started drinking it. Oddly, she was a little nervous because she didn't know if he asked her there to try to make a move on her or if they were still in that drinking buddy stage. She didn't care one way or another; she just wanted to know if she needed to slam the drink and leave, because she needed to work in the morning, or was she going to spend the night? Alex had three main things on the brain, drinking, sex, and sleep. She needed all three of them, they were important, if she wasn't getting the sex from Peter Pan, she needed to go home to take care of it herself. She didn't mind going home and taking care of herself, she wasn't called the toy lady for nothing.

Alex had three treasure chests full of sex toys, lotions, and potions. If anyone needed bedroom advice, whether it be to try something new, or if there was an issue in the lovemaking department, Alex was happy to give advice and suggestions. She felt like it was her calling to help people enjoy their sex lives and not think of it as dirty. When she was 17-years-old, she got her first vibrator. She was hooked and began collecting sex toys ever since. She spent so much money, that she decided to be a sex toy party lady as soon as she turned 18.

Peter Pan must have read her mind, because as soon as she was done with her white Russian, Peter Pan took the glass out of her hand, placed it on the side table next to him, and attacked. They were in his living room- the curtains were open and everyone, if anyone was actually awake and looking, would have gotten quite the show. Peter Pan pressed Alex against the wall, picked her up, and he kissed her. It was passionate. She was taken off guard but thought –*Ok, here we go Peter Pan, hold on.* She honestly didn't think he had it in him, but YES he did. He said, "I have been wanting to do this since the first night we played pool together." He started stripping her down right in the living room as he continued to kiss her. She was down to her bra and panties. He looked at her and said, "Wow, red is my favorite color." Alex was wearing red laced bra and panties. Alex laughed and began ripping off Peter Pan's clothes. She unbuttoned his pants and pulled them down. He was wearing black boxer briefs. Alex said, "Crazy, black happens to be my favorite color." He picked her up and carried her into his bedroom. He vigorously tossed Alex on the bed, on top of a lacrosse stick, Alex laughed. She never saw that side of Peter Pan before. He was kind of rough but yet still playful. He quickly threw the lacrosse stick on the floor and climbed on top of Alex. They continued to make out. It was intense. Alex said, "You're a bit aggressive Peter Pan." He responded, "Yeah when I want something, I go for it." He continued to kiss her. Her flower swelled. She pulled down his boxers, "There's the Monster" she said. He laughed and growled playfully saying, "He is a Monster. He has been lurking with anticipation of attacking you for some time now." They laughed and continued to kiss. He took off her bra and panties. He looked her straight in the eyes while he put on a condom and gently put himself inside her. They both moaned, he began to thrust inside her slowly and gently.

He paid attention to her every move, her every moan, if she moaned a certain way, he knew what she liked, and he kept hitting that spot. Sex was a sport, and Peter Pan was good at sports. He was very verbal which surprised Alex. When he was on top of her if she moaned, he would say, "Yeah, you like that?" And if she answered yeah, he would moan back "yeah." He would pump into her and say "Yeah? Yeah?" and he would have this high pitch sound to his voice. She thought it was funny, but it turned her on too. He did a pelvic thrust as he went in and out of her he would twist his hip just right, and she was gone. She started to climax, gushing all over him, screaming with excitement. He climaxed and let out this loud moan as he came. He looked at her with eyes of passion and kissed her for what seemed like forever and then he rolled over to lay by her side. He looked up at the ceiling and said, "I have to tell you, I love all your smells. I even like that cherry lime-aid air freshener you have in your car. You always smell amazing, when you hug me, the smell of you stays on my clothes and I never want to wash them. Just now, I could not wait to kiss you out in the living-room, because I know you put on different flavored lip gloss every time we hang out. I always want to know what flavor you have on and how it tastes, every time I see you. You excite me." Then he looked at her and said, "It tasted like chocolate." She laughed and said, "MMMM… close, the flavor of my lip gloss tonight is Marshmello Chocolate Mocha." Yep, he got more verbal that night.

Chapter 35

Alex and Peter Pan continued to have sleepovers and shortly after their first overnight, he asked her if she wanted to go to Florida with him. He got a good deal on a resort and he had a limited time to use it. She didn't know if she should go or not. He told her not to worry, it was just a fun trip he didn't want to go on his own to. He assured her it didn't mean anything serious. She agreed to go but only if he would do one thing for her. She wanted him to send down her sex swing. She had purchased a sex swing and wanted to try it out. She didn't want it at her place just in case her parents came over, and he couldn't have it at his place because he was renting, and he didn't want any issues with his landlord. He agreed to mail the sex swing to the Florida resort when it was time for their trip. He laughed. He liked that she liked trying something new, and he loved it whenever she got new toys. Peter Pan really liked it when she got new toys for couples or any oil and lotions because she would try them out with him. He was the perfect guinea pig. He was so vocal, he would tell her what he thought, and for sure what he liked.

Peter Pan would often text Alex while she was at work asking her what his favorite color of the day was, and that meant he wanted to know what color panties she was wearing. It always made Alex blush when she got that text. Peter Pan liked that she was adventurous and used sex as her way of acting out. Often, while at work, she would message him "afternoon delight" which meant he needed to find a bathroom, text her the location, and she would meet him, and they would have a quickie in the bathroom. That was his mission. He liked it when she sent him on missions. He needed to be careful, it needed to be a private, single-stall bathroom, and no cameras. They didn't need to lose their jobs over their sexcapades. He would always find the perfect bathroom, ones that she never even knew existed.

Peter Pan was always up for anything and Alex loved that about him. Sometimes she would show up at his house wearing costumes and they would role-play together. There was one time she had him wearing a black bowtie and bikini briefs that looked like a tuxedo and she demanded him make her drinks wearing them all night. He eventually stripteased down to just wearing the bowtie. He danced for Alex and she couldn't stand it. He was so sweet and playful and would do anything she asked, she usually gave in too quickly on role-playing nights and they would end up having sex within the hour. Sometimes she would show up in S&M leather outfits with belts and straps. She would order him to strip down to nothing and make him pose in certain positions, and he would do it. She loved how submissive he was. She felt bad because sometimes she thought she went too far. He would literally do anything she asked or commanded. She tried multiple S&M devices on him and even though he didn't like it he would allow her to try it out. One night she even tried erotic asphyxiation with a belt while they were having sex just to see if she could get him to a higher level of intense orgasms. His face turned shades of red, his eyes started to water and he didn't fight her, it freaked her out, she loosened the belt and quickly took it off him. Her eyes were filled with tears, she couldn't stand the thought of hurting him, and the fact that he would allow her to do it. She kissed him and apologized. She told him no more S&M. He smiled and kissed her. She said the only thing she would do is call him a bad boy when he was out of line. They both laughed and he kissed her passionately. She hugged him tight and said, "Seriously, I'm so sorry Peter Pan you've been a good boy. You can do whatever you want to me." He smiled and crawled under the sheets and opened up her legs and made love to her flower with his mouth. She moaned, "Oh, you are such a good boy." He giggled and then within seconds she moaned in ecstasy as she squirted all over him.

Chapter 36

Peter Pan asked Alex to go with him up to his parent's place for a long weekend. Alex wasn't sure about going, meeting family was kind of a no-no. Peter Pan begged and said even though she would be meeting his parents, tons of his friends have met his parents, it wasn't anything serious, it would just be a fun weekend. Alex had heard stories about Peter Pan's parent's home, she kind of wanted to check it out, so she decided to go. It was almost an eight-hour drive. On the drive there, Peter Pan admitted that it was actually his parent's wedding anniversary weekend and that his sister would be stopping by for a couple of days too. But once again, it wasn't going to be anything serious.

His parent's cabin looked like something you would see in a magazine. Peter Pan said his parents designed the house and handpicked every piece of wood, they even carved their names and the date they built the house on one of the mainboards in the living room. It was one of the first things she noticed when she walked into the great room. Their house was an A-frame log house, six bedrooms, and three bathrooms, it was huge and open with giant windows and a wraparound porch, sitting right on the lake. It was the most beautiful view Alex had ever seen.

When Peter Pan and Alex arrived at his parent's place, his parents came out to welcome them with big warm hugs. Peter Pan's family was Italian, very loving and fun. Peter Pan's mom wanted them to make spaghetti by hand and showed Alex her kitchen. They rolled out the dough by hand and made the spaghetti sauce by hand as well. Alex thought it took way too long. It was tradition to drink wine while cooking. Alex said that Peter Pan's mom was nice and funny, but very particular when it came to cooking. Needless to say; there was probably a little more wine than normal in the spaghetti sauce. Peter Pan's mom kept filling Alex's wine class and asking Alex and Peter Pan questions about their relationship, how they met, she even asked Alex if Peter Pan was a good kisser. Alex just laughed. Peter Pan's mom said that Alex was the first girl he had brought home. Alex was surprised by that because he had mentioned that he brought other friends up to the cabin, but they must have all been guy friends. Alex was a bit tipsy by the time the spaghetti was actually done and ready to eat, she feared that she talked way too much to Peter Pan's mom.

Alex liked his family and loved the little jokes they shared and how loving they were to one another and even to Alex. Peter Pan's sister arrived the following day. They ended up going boating and jet skiing all day. When they came back to the cabin Peter Pan went on a walk with his mom and his sister, while Alex rested in the hammock on the porch and listened to some music while she took in all the feels. She was listening to music by Angus and Julia Stone and fell asleep. Peter Pan's dad took nightly walks by the lake and he walked by where Alex was sleeping, he hummed along to the music and laid a soft blanket over her, and then kept walking. Alex felt him put the warm blanket on her and heard him humming, she instantly fell in love. She loved his parents. Later that night the whole family went into town. They went to some local bars for dinner and drinks. They bar hopped and even did some karaoke. As a group, they sang *Sweet Caroline* and *Friends in Low Places*. Alex said she never laughed so hard in her life. She said she would never have that experience with her own parents.

Alex even met Peter Pan's grandma who was an immigrant from Italy. They played cards and had cookies with tea. Grandma talked to Peter Pan and Alex about love and told them all about her tormented love life. When she was a girl, she fell in love with a boy from her village, but her parents promised her to another. She was forced to marry the man her parents wanted her to marry. After she got married, she and her new husband moved to the United States. His grandma was heartbroken and terrified, she married a stranger, moved away from her family, from the man she loved, and moved to a completely new country, not speaking the language or anything. She said she would call the boy she loved back home and as soon as the boy would pick up the phone and say hello she would hang up. She just wanted to hear his voice, and she wanted him to know she was ok. She said the man she was forced to marry was an alcoholic and abusive. Life was hard but she had a family with him. She loved her children but never forgot about the boy she loved, and she called him every month, just to hang up after he answered the phone. Alex wanted to know what happened with the boy back home, was he still alive? Because Peter Pan's grandpa was gone, he had been gone for decades. Peter Pan never got to know his grandfather. Peter Pan's grandma said that she still calls her love in Italy and they talk on the phone, but they are both too old and frail to travel so, unfortunately, they will never see each other again. Alex thought that was so tragic. She could not believe that someone hasn't gotten them together. Grandma wanted to know how serious Alex and Peter Pan were and Peter Pan explained that they were just close friends. Grandma was not buying it. Alex thought Peter Pan's grandma was cute but feisty and Alex got the feeling that Grandma didn't really approve of her.

When Alex and Peter Pan got back to the cabin, Peter Pan's parents were making dinner together. They talked to Peter Pan's parents about their visit with grandma for a while. Alex told Peter Pan she was going to quickly pack up and then take a shower before they ate. They were going to go home after dinner, so she wanted to make sure she got a shower before the long drive home. Peter Pan quickly said he would show her how to use the shower because it was very tricky, and he followed her to the bathroom. They walked into the bathroom and Alex asked him what was so tricky about the shower. He laughed and said there was nothing tricky about it. All Alex had to do was turn the handle left or right for hot or cold, and up and down for on or off. She looked at him like he was nuts and he laughed. He said he just wanted to be with her alone. He kissed her and said, "We haven't done it in this bathroom, and look, no cameras, it's private and single-stall." He had a little boy's grin on his face. He took off his shirt and started unbuttoning his pants, then he kissed her again, and then again more passionately. Alex laughed and said, "Oh Monster wants to come out and play? Maybe we better lock the door." Peter Pan laughed and then quickly locked the door.

Chapter 37

It had been six weeks since Alex and Peter Pan visited his parents. Alex was pleasantly surprised that the weekend trip to his folk's place didn't cause their relationship to get awkward or change in any way. They continued to hang out regularly, going to games, sports bars, dart league, having sleepovers, and meeting each other in random bathrooms. One morning, Alex received a text from Peter Pan that read, "Package has landed and arrived at destination." Meaning the sex swing would be at the resort when they check-in. They were flying out to Florida that night after work and she was so excited. They got to the resort, checked in and Peter Pan asked for the package. The hotel receptionist told him it was delivered to the room already. Alex's eyes bulged out of her head. She hoped no one actually opened the package. They went up to the room and the package was still wrapped in the packing box. Alex thought, *shew*. They checked out the room. It was a suite that had a balcony that overlooked the pool and the ocean in the distance. It was beautiful. She looked at Peter Pan and said she wanted the swing on the balcony. When it started getting dark out, she wanted to have sex on the balcony. He said ok. They waited until it got close to dark before hanging the swing up, they didn't want to get busted. Peter Pan turned on the song *Slow Hands* by Niall Horan. They both drank a few glasses of captain to get their liquid courage up, they danced and started making out. They were both turned on and were ready to try the swing. They were clumsy at first but then they got the hang of it. It wasn't the most comfortable thing and they swung into the wall a couple of times and laughed their asses off, eventually, they were able to get the job done. She thought it might be better for a pregnant woman. She could bend over, having her belly in the swing and the man could come up behind her and gently swing her into him. They tried the swing again inside the room, but they quickly stopped. Alex decided the sex swing was a fun fantasy, but it didn't work out that great. That's why she liked to try everything out before recommending it to other people and Peter Pan was a perfect sport about it.

The next morning Alex woke up to the sound of rain. Peter Pan was sitting out on the balcony drinking coffee with baileys, Juice Wrld playing softly in the background, and she could see that Peter Pan was filling up the hot tub that was out on the balcony. She walked out onto the balcony, and he smiled at her. He dumped all the travel-sized shampoo bottles that were in the hotel, into the hot tub. The suds started overflowing, they were flowing over the balcony onto the balconies below them, and on the yard below. Soap-suds were flowing out onto the grass and towards the pool area. Peter Pan looked at Alex and they both laughed. He handed her a mimosa and they both stripped down to nothing and got into the hot tub. He called it their private foam party.

They were supposed to go snorkeling that day but because of all the rain, they were unable to go. They lounged around for a while in town but then later that night they ended up going on a party cruise. She was wearing a bright blue tube top and black mini skirt with high chunky black sandals. He was dressed in dark jeans and a black polo shirt. Peter Pan's bright blue eyes popped when he wore black. Alex loved it. When Peter Pan purchased the tickets, the girl who waited on him upgraded him to VIP access for free. That meant they got top-shelf booze and the surf and turf dinner, included with their access. He was always lucky like that. They danced on the top deck of the boat. Peter Pan even persuaded some of the wait staff to join him in on the cupid shuffle. Alex loved dancing and she loved watching Peter Pan goof off. He always knew how to create a party atmosphere.

The party cruise was over at 11:00 PM. Peter Pan wanted to hit up Duvall Street before they went back to their room. They walked up and down Duvall Street, going from bar to bar, dancing, and having a blast. Peter Pan noticed that Alex's feet were bleeding where the sandal straps were. They must have been digging into her feet most of the night. He asked her about it, and she said she was fine. He said, "You're not fine, you're bleeding. You're fucking bleeding!" She didn't know what the big deal was, she told him she would soak her feet when they got back to their room, they were having fun and she didn't want her feet to ruin their night. He looked at her all pissed, "I want you to tell me when you are hurt. I want you to tell me things, have a fucking opinion." She looked at him shocked and asked him where all this was coming from. He said, "Last week when you weren't feeling good, I told you to come over and I would make you chicken noodle soup. We stayed in and watched Netflix instead of going out to watch the game with my buddies. We had soup, and I asked you what you wanted to watch. You said you didn't care. I picked *Fever Pitch*. You said that was fine. When I asked you how you liked it, you said you thought it was cute, but it wouldn't be a movie you would have picked. You wouldn't have picked a romantic comedy. What would you have picked? You don't tell me what you like, you don't have a fucking opinion, you just do whatever I want to do and go along with whatever. Your fucking feet are bleeding Alex! Yell at me and tell me to stop dragging you from bar to bar and take you back to the room. Call me a dick, I don't care. Say something!" She looked at him and said, "I like Rocky Road ice cream. Last week you asked me what kind of ice cream I liked, and I said any kind, but I'm letting you know right now, my favorite kind is Rocky Road. Romantic comedies are fine, but I am drawn to action, crime, and psychological thrillers. I think you and your sister have some sick, twisted relationship. I don't know if she wants you to be her sister or her fuckfriend. I honestly think she wants to fuck you. And it totally pisses me off when she calls you 'BITCH' or 'Stacey', you're not a girl. She's obnoxious. What did I forget? OH, and my feet are fucking killing me. Let's go back to the resort, you Dick!" She was red in the face, and then smiled a huge guilty grin like she said way too much. He looked at her and said, "Thank God! Thank YOU!" He picked her up and carried her all the way back to the resort.

The next day they spent most of the day by the pool. Alex couldn't go into the ocean because the saltwater hurt her feet too bad. They had the red-eye flight that night. The flight home was quiet. Peter Pan was quiet. When they arrived back in town, they went to their own houses.

Peter Pan texted her the next day saying that the sex swing was delivered to his house. She could come and get it anytime or she could leave it, he just wanted to let her know. She thanked him and then asked him if he wanted to meet up later for drinks. They met at Buffalo Wild Wings. Alex was happy that sports were on every TV, it made the awkward silence less awkward between her and Peter Pan. Alex was worried that Peter Pan was too attached. She didn't want to hurt him. He was a great guy and she enjoyed hanging out with him, but once again, she didn't think it was fair to drag out what they were doing. He deserved more and she knew he wanted more. He made it obvious on the Florida trip. He deserved a girl that was going to have an opinion and share her likes, dislikes, and her life with him. Alex knew she wasn't ready for that.

Chapter 38

Sadie voiced that she was always disappointed with the Florida story, she was hoping the sex swing would have gotten confiscated by hotel security. Alex laughed and said that definitely would have made it more interesting. Jeff came by and Keira ordered another round, Alex wanted a Captain this time. Jeff said, "A Captain with enough limes to make a palm tree?" He winked at her, "coming up" and walked away. Keira looked at Alex and said, "You haven't quit Anaconda yet have you?" Alex laughed and said, "I don't think I ever want to shake Anaconda, he's about as good as it's going to get." Keira knew what she meant, as far as what Alex was saying she wanted and needed right now, he was perfect. He was young, Alex loved spending time with him, and he was not going to get attached. Anaconda and Alex made a pact that it was friends with benefits and that's all. Alex learned her lesson, and Anaconda just got out of a bad, long-term relationship, long term for a 24-year-old that is, and he wasn't ready for anything. Jess and Sadie piped in, "Who the hell is Anaconda?" Alex only told Keira about him. She wanted to keep that one on the down-low and private. Keira quickly responded, "Oh you know Alex, she likes keeping randoms on the string." The girls laughed.

Anaconda

Anaconda played kickball, softball, and beach volleyball with four of Alex's co-workers. He worked at the same hospital, but he worked in Gastroenterology. He was young, 24-years-young. He was tall and thin, and his head was shaved. He lived in a big Victorian house six blocks away from the hospital, with three guy housemates. After their games, Anaconda and his friends would host house parties. The house parties consisted of people just showing up, listening to music, drinking, and socializing. Alex only checked out the party once because it reminded her of a frat house. Her co-worker, Shelly, begged her to go because she liked one of Anaconda's roommates and didn't want to go alone.

Alex and Shelly walked into the party and grabbed a couple of beers. There were people all over the house, in the kitchen, in the hall, in the living room and she thought most likely in the bedrooms too. There were probably at least 30 people there. They were playing a variety of rap and hip hop music like Lil Wayne, Eminem, Pop Smoke, Young Thug, Fetty Wap, Ty Dolla $ign, G-Eazy, Juice Wrld, MGK, etc. Alex liked the music. She walked into the living room where there were a few people she knew there. They all worked at the hospital but in different departments. Anaconda was sitting on the couch talking with a group of people and he mentioned that he worked in gastroenterology, Alex overheard him saying, "It was an okay job if you like working with assholes." Everyone in the room laughed. He was funny. Alex actually thought he was really cute. She liked his spunky personality. Alex stayed and drank a couple of beers but then saw that Shelly was hitting it off with some people at the party. She told Shelly she was going to head home. Shelly gave her a hug bye and said she would see her at work in the morning.

The following day Alex got an email from Anaconda. He said he noticed her at the party with Shelly and wanted to know why she left so soon. Alex wrote him back and said it was a great party, great people, great music, great booze she just needed to go home to work on homework. That was always her excuse when she needed to bail, "homework." Alex and Anaconda emailed each other back and forth all day. She learned he was in school for his master's in hospital administration. They both found out that the other person was single, and he told her about his last relationship. He was still pretty bitter about it. His ex-girlfriend was a party girl and everything he wanted in a girl, she was hot and knew how to have a good time. She was into sports like he was. She was great at volleyball and softball. Apparently, she was super smart and was going to school for marketing. She was a couple of years younger than him and was really enjoying college life. They went to different colleges which made life tough for them. She liked to play around. She was not faithful, and she had every excuse in the book why she strayed. She was either drunk, or she missed him and was lonely, it was one reason after another. She went on a lot of girl trips and he couldn't trust her. She would send videos of her and her friends topless in bars and he said he had enough. It was driving him crazy. He couldn't put up with it anymore. He finally dumped her. She came crawling back and he took her back, only for her to fuck him over again. He said he was never going to put himself through that again. It sucked. The not being able to trust her sucked. He couldn't sleep, he was worried about where she was, who she was with, and what she was doing. Alex was sympathetic and told him that apparently, his ex wasn't as smart as he thought she was. However; Alex said in the ex's defense, being young and out in the world for the first time, it's hard to live by rules, and if she was as hot as he says, the temptation was everywhere, and mixing parties with that, drinking and what else…. GOOD LUCK. It would be rare for a relationship to survive under those circumstances. It's too bad the ex, couldn't be honest with Anaconda, letting him know that she just wanted to experience college life and play around. She should have gotten out of the relationship gracefully, instead of looking like a crazy party slut. Alex told him his ex was an idiot, and one day she'll regret how the relationship ended. She told him the good news was he was young and eventually the right girl would come along, blow him away, and the ex will just be a pain in the ass from the past.

He heard through the grapevine that Alex was a widow but didn't know if she was dating someone or not. He said he had seen her out at some sports bars with a guy and didn't know if it was her boyfriend. She assumed he was talking about Peter Pan. She was honest with Anaconda and told him they were basically just hanging out as friends or friends with benefits. He was not her boyfriend. And in fact, she told him she hadn't hung out with him for a while because he wanted something more than what she could give. She was not ready for something like that. She said she was still a mess and not right for anyone at the present. He said he was a mess too. They enjoyed emailing back and forth so much that Alex started calling him names like Cue-Ball and Youngin', he seemed to like it. He called her Sweetmess, and she liked that too. They emailed daily, all day for weeks and Alex always looked forward to hearing from him.

Chapter 39

One day Anaconda sent Alex an email saying that his housemates were stuck working overnights that week and wanted to know if Alex wanted to come over to his place and chill. She said sure. She thought he was great, they had great conversations and they were interested in a lot of the same things. He told her to show up any time after 5:00 and he would be home. Alex texted him at 6:00 and said she was on her way.

Alex showed up at his place, knocked on the door and he opened it a few seconds later. He seemed taller than she remembered. He had to be at least 6 feet. He was thin and she loved his bald head. He was dressed in baggy light grey sweatpants and a white muscle shirt, that was form-fitting. She could see he had a 6-pack and well-defined muscle tone. He looked at her, smiled, and opened the door wide, "Hey Alex." Alex felt flushed. She was very attracted to him. She smiled and said, "Hey Cue-Ball." He smiled and said, "Come on in. Can I get you something to drink?" She asked him if he had Captain and he said, "Sure, of course." He wanted to know what she would like with it, she said diet coke would be great if he had it, and he did. He made her a drink and then asked her if she was hungry. He bragged about being a gourmet cook and said he was making Kraft mac and cheese and was willing to share if she was interested. They both laughed. They talked for a while in his kitchen while he was making his dinner and Alex felt pretty comfortable. He was a regular guy, no pressure. He wasn't flirtatious, he was just very matter of fact and she liked that. He wasn't trying to pretend he was something he was not. After they were done eating, he asked Alex if she would like to see the rest of the house since no one else was there. It was a five-bedroom, three-bathroom house. It had three floors, and his room was on the top floor which was basically a loft apartment, it was very large, open and he had his own bathroom. It was nice.

He showed her around his bedroom, it was a quick tour, he pointed out the bathroom, and then he showed her where he slept. He had a big bed and a huge ass flat-screen TV. Pretty simple, she liked it. He looked at her and said, "I don't have any chairs, just the bed, and you're welcome to sit on the bed but I do have one rule. If you are going to get IN the bed, no pants are allowed." She looked at him and said, "No pants are allowed IN your bed? So, if I wanted to crawl under the covers with you, I have to take my pants off?" He looked at her seriously, nodding his head, and said, "You can leave your underwear on. I just don't like pants in my bed. It's a rule." She laughed and said, "OK, fair enough, no pants on in the bed." He nodded. He asked her if she would like to watch a movie and she said sure. He asked her what she thought about *The Boondock Saints*? She got excited and said, "It's a classic." He smiled and agreed, he said it was one of his favorites. He turned the movie on, and he took off his sweatpants and crawled into bed. He did it so fast that Alex didn't even see him do it. He looked up at her as if he was asking her what's it going to be? She thought to herself, I guess it's time for me to take my pants off. She unbuttoned her jeans and slid them off. She was wearing red laced booty shorts, matching red laced bra, and a red fitted MGK t-shirt. He lifted up his sheets and comforter so she could crawl in. He moved back and pulled her closer to him. They were both laying on their side watching the movie. He asked her if she was comfortable and she was. He was very warm, and his sheets smelt clean, he smelt clean, she just felt very comfortable. He wrapped his arm around her holding her and she really liked it. He moved her hair away from her neck, leaving her neck exposed, and continued to watch the movie. Her hair must have been in the way of his vision because he didn't bend down to kiss her. She was kind of disappointed. About halfway into the movie she had to get up and go to the bathroom. She went into the bathroom. It was a clean, small bathroom with a toilet, sink, and shower, nothing fancy but it was perfect for a young, single guy.

She walked back into his room and he lifted the blankets again to let her in. This time she crawled in and faced him. He held her close to him and said "Hey Sweetmess" she said "Hey" back. She looked at his mouth and saw a scar above his upper lip. She touched it with her finger and asked him if there was a good story behind that scar. He said not really. It was something that happened to him as a kid, he and his cousin were messing around and he ran into a shelf face first. The shelf had a sharp edge and cut him right there. It left a scar. He said he wished he had a better story like he was in a bar fight and some guy smacked him with a glass bottle or something. He laughed. Alex touched the scar again, and then she kissed it. He let her kiss it. He smiled and just looked back at her. She kissed it again and then kissed him on his mouth. He kissed her back. He then kissed her bottom lip and started kissing her neck. He came back up and kissed her on the lips, kissing her passionately. He rolled over on his back and he lifted her on top of him. They continued to kiss. She was laying on top of him, gliding her body across his. She could feel his erection. It was long and so hard. Her flower was starting to swell, and she was getting wet with excitement. He was an amazing kisser and the way he touched her, made her body tingle all over, it was a thrilling sensation. She ended up taking off her t-shirt, and as she did, he took his off too. They continued to kiss and rub their bodies against one another. She loved laying on top of his body, she loved kissing him, his lips, his neck his bald head. They must have made out for a good 45 minutes, kissing and grinding. She was breathing heavily. She was excited and wanted to work down his body with her mouth. She started moving her body down his body. She kissed his lips, neck, and chest. She started kissing down his mid-section and saw that he had some sort of tribal tattoo up the right side of his ribcage. It was fucking sexy as hell. She licked and kissed it. As she licked it, he twitched. He laughed but seemed turned on by it. She continued to lick and kiss it. She saw he was wearing grey and black camo boxer briefs. She dragged her tongue across the band of his briefs, and then pulled them off. She saw it. She saw his cock and said out loud "Anaconda." He laughed and said, "What?" She looked at him, bright-eyed, and said, "Your cock is perfect, it's long and thick, it's so beautiful." She went down on him. Taking her time dragging her tongue all up and down his big beautiful cock, she stroked his cock while she was sucking it, pushing him in and out of her mouth. He grabbed his headboard, his legs got stiff and he let out a loud groan. He came in her mouth. He came a lot. His cum was so sweet. She thought it must be all the grape Gatorade he drinks. She read that depending on the guy's diet, their cum can taste sweet, salty, or sour. She heard that guys who ate more lemons have sweeter-tasting cum. Well, they should probably add grape Gatorade to the list of things one should be feeding their guy.

He looked at her as if he was thunderstruck and pulled her up closer to him and kissed her. He kissed her passionately. He held her and rolled her over so that she was lying on her back and he was on top of her. He reciprocated. He kissed her body starting from her lips, all the way down to her red lace panties. He pulled them off, opening up her legs. He dragged the tip of his tongue down to her flower and it was as if he consumed her. She grabbed his bald head and wanted him to stay down there forever. He felt so good. While his head was between her legs his hands were fondling her breasts and her nipples. Her nipples were so hard, she started moaning and her legs were shaking, she started having orgasmic convulsions. She cried out in ecstasy and she came all over. She gushed on his face. She needed that so much. Fuck he was amazing. He slowly crawled up her body, kissing her body on the way up. He grabbed his Gatorade, took a drink, and offered Alex some. She took a couple of sips. He kissed her and then curled up beside her, spooning her. They fell asleep. A few hours later Alex woke up. She rolled out of bed and got dressed. He looked at her and told her she didn't have to leave. His roommates wouldn't be home until 7:00 that morning. She said it was ok, she would message him later.

Chapter 40

When Alex got to work, she saw that Anaconda already emailed her. It read, "Did you name my dick Anaconda?" She emailed him back, "Yes!" He wrote back, "Will you be coming back over?" She said she could swing by later that night if he wanted her to. He wrote back, "Awesome" with a smiley face.

Alex texted him saying she would be there by 6:00. When she arrived, he opened the door and he welcomed her in. He was wearing black sweats and no shirt. He was so delicious looking. Every time she saw him, she got butterflies. He offered her a drink. They talked about their workday and walked up to his room. He had Kings of Leon playing softly in the background. He dropped his pants and crawled into bed. Alex dropped her pants and crawled in right after him. They continued to talk about their day, drank a little, and just laid there visiting. They were facing each other. He had chameleon eyes, sometimes they were green, sometimes they were blue. She liked them, she liked everything about Youngin'. She was tracing the tattoo on his ribcage with her finger and said she was thinking about his tattoo all day. He asked her if she liked it. She said she did. She wanted to know if he was thinking about getting more. He said he would like another one. He wanted the words 'zieht eure Schwerter' tattooed on him, which translated to 'draw your swords' in German. She said, "OOOO....are you going to put that on your back across your shoulder blades?" She thought that sounded so hot. He said he was thinking of putting it across his upper chest, above his heart. He wanted to be able to see it. He said it was ridiculous to spend money on a tattoo you never get to see. Alex nodded in agreement but still thought back tattoos were hot, especially on the right people.

He said he noticed she was a tattoo virgin. He asked her if she would ever get a tattoo? She said she thought about it all the time. She laughed and said her inner self wants her body to be covered with tattoos, but she only knows of one lady that can pull something like that off, creating a tasteful and sexy look. Unfortunately, Alex was certain it would not look good on her little body. He wanted to know what she would get tattooed on her body and where. She said she would get the words 'Feel the Feels' on the inside of her right bicep. She also would want to be covered in stars. On her neck, on her ribcage, down to her feet, little and big stars. She had the image of her twirling around and with every twirl, she made you could see a star somewhere on her body. But then she went on to say she couldn't get stars without an angel or two, maybe three, because stars and angels should always be together. She wanted an angel in chains, surrounded by her big damaged, broken down wings. The angel would have no face but long hair, and a tilted or broken halo. A priest all in black would be behind the angel embracing her with his body, trying to hold her up and unhooking her from her chains. The priest's embrace is sensual, a desire to help the angel with all his might. Their faces so close, as if they are kissing. Alex went on to say she wanted another angel that was not broken but strong, walking with a big gorgeous lion. The lion would be wearing a crown with jewels and a red heart on it. The angel would be beautiful, still faceless, with long flowing hair, her wings so big and full of life, dragging to the ground as she walks with the lion. There would be a third faceless angel, with long hair, and big beautiful wings, she'll be holding onto a bright, beautiful, perfect star. The angel will be lifting the star up to the sky, and light would shine all around them. Alex said she would also get a back tattoo across her shoulders that would be the words 'Jigsaw Girl'. Anaconda asked what that was referenced to, and she said it was a song by the Toadies, it was just her, she was Jigsaw Girl. She said it was hard to explain. She felt like she was a puzzle with lots of pieces, she never knew if she was going to be whole again. Anaconda smiled a sad smile as he nodded. Alex continued saying of course she would get a tattoo with the saying 'When you're gone, you're still a part of me'. She didn't know where she would put that, maybe on her lower back, or on her collar bone, above her heart, she didn't know. But they all meant something to her, and she would want them all. She laughed and said, "You see why I can't start, I would never stop, and I would be covered." She looked at him and told him he needed an anaconda tattoo. He looked at her and laughed and said, "Maybe YOU should get an anaconda tattoo?". She said, "Where do you suggest I put it, around my finger?" She smiled. He tickled her and replied, "I was thinking wrap that big bitch around your whole body."

She laughed and said, " OH? You want to suffocate me?" Still laughing, she looked at his lips, she wanted to kiss him. She saw that scar above his lip. She loved that scar. She thought it was so sexy. She kissed the scar. She then kissed him on the lips. She kissed him again more deeply the second time. He kissed her back. But he was holding back a little, she could tell. She kissed him again and started rubbing her body up against his and she felt his hard cock bulging through his boxers. She wanted to touch him so bad. She wanted to feel him inside her. He moved Alex on her back, and he continued to kiss her while his body grinded upon hers. It was as if they were having sex with their underwear on. She could feel him up against her flower, pressing on it. She was wet. He was wet. She started whining and moaning. He looked into her eyes and said softly, "What do you want?" She looked at him with her bedroom eyes. And she started pulling at his boxer briefs. He stopped rubbing against her body and said, "What do you want Alex? Use your words." He continued to rub up and down her body, kissing her neck, and her lips passionately. She continued to moan and whine. She started moving her hand down to his boxers so she could feel him. He was so hard, and she started stroking him with his briefs on. He was breathing heavily. He looked at her, and said, "Uh uh- you have to use your words." As he continued to rub on her and kiss her. She stroked his cock and she cried out, "I want you. I want you inside me." He leaned back and she could see his enormous, hard, thick, and long dick bulging in his boxers. He slid his boxers off, and Anaconda came out. He reached up and grabbed a condom and Alex's flower was swollen with excitement, she was so wet. He put the condom on, and he put the tip of anaconda inside her. He said, "You want this? Is this what you wanted?"

She moaned yes and he slowly slid inside her. They both moaned loudly. He whispered in Alex's ear "Fuck, you feel so good." She was thinking the same about him, but she could not speak. He continued to push into her, back and forth. He felt amazing. It was like she was transcending. She yelled out a long moan as she climaxed, and he moaned with her. He pushed into her harder and he let out a loud moan as he came. He kissed her on the forehead and then her lips and cheek and then he rolled over. He turned, looked at her and he said, "Holy fuck." She looked at him and said, "Holy fuck is right Youngin'." They laid there for a while, and then Alex got up, got dressed, kissed him, and said she would talk to him later.

Chapter 41

They saw each other a lot. He would text her the snake emoji whenever he wanted to see her. Every time she saw it, she got excited. Sometimes they would go to his house over lunchtime if he knew his housemates would be gone. She could not get enough of him. She told Keira there was one time she was at her cousin's wedding, which was out of town; she got a text from Anaconda and she left as early as she could, drove 2 ½ hours just to be with him.

One evening Alex went to a Saving Abel concert with a couple of her girlfriends. Her friend won free backstage passes to meet the band at the end of the show. Alex was lit up, she was well primmed with drinks and the stimulation from the music. She met, took pictures with, and got autographs from the band. Alex was on cloud 9. She texted Anaconda the snake emoji with a question mark. She knew his housemates were home, but she didn't care. He texted back, "What are you waiting for? Come get some." Alex immediately got excited.

Alex showed up at the house and Anaconda was waiting at the door for her, with a captain in hand, just for her. He asked her how the concert was. She said it was amazing. She felt energized and needed to work off some excess energy. He smiled. She walked in the door and there were a few people over having drinks, engaged in some serious gaming activities. They didn't even seem to notice that she walked into the house. Anaconda grabbed her by the hand and walked her up to his room. He looked at Alex, licked his lips, and said, "I like the leather pants." He slapped her in the ass and said, "It's a shame you have to take them off." She asked him what he was doing, and he looked down at books and his laptop, he was working on a paper for school. He moved his books and laptop and put them on the floor. He took off his pants and sat on his bed and pulled Alex closer to him. Her leather pants were held up by one zipper. He unzipped it and slid her pants off. She was wearing black laced thongs. He grabbed her ass and licked his lips again and said, "Good God Sweetmess, look what you do to me!" Anaconda was hard, he was oh so hard. She straddled him. She took off her tank. She was wearing a black and silver-laced bra. He started kissing her breasts, and then he took off her bra. He kissed her more passionately and rolled her over on her back. He kept kissing her on her lips and then he whispered, "Saving Abel, right?" She said, "Yeah." He started singing in her ear, "I'm so addicted to… all the things you do," he continued to kiss her, moving down her body "when you're going down on me… in between the sheets," moving down her body some more, "Oh, the sounds you make, with every breath you take," kissing and caressing her breasts, and then moving down to her panties, and continued to sing, "It's unlike anything… when you're loving me." He took her panties off and he opened up her legs and started kissing her down there. She started to moan, her back arched, her legs twitched, she started having convulsions, she cried out as she exploded all over. When she was done, he kissed her stomach, her breasts, and then he kissed her face and lips. He said, "You literally smell and taste like peaches." She smiled and said," It's a new peaches and cream edible lotion. Do you like it? Is it ok?" He smiled and nodded, as he kissed her passionately. She heard him grab a condom and rip the package open. He placed himself inside her and he fucked her deep and smooth. He did a graceful pelvic thrust deep into her. It was erotic. He felt so amazing she couldn't get enough, she felt bewitched by him. They both moaned loudly as he continued to thrust into her. She cried out, he kissed her deeply and hard, he pumped into her again and again and he moaned loudly and yelled out "FUCK!" as he came and then he kissed her again passionately. He slid himself out of her and rolled over, continuing to kiss her. It was intense and alarming how good they felt together. Their sexual chemistry was off the charts and they both knew it. She looked at him and said, "How are we ever going to stop doing this?" He just stared at her and then kissed her some more.

Chapter 42

One night, Alex went out to a local bar with some girlfriends from work. Anaconda happened to be out with some buddies at the same bar. All the friends somewhat knew each other, so Alex and her friends grabbed drinks and went over to Anaconda's table of friends to say hi. Alex and Anaconda just looked at each other and said casual hellos. They didn't get close to each other. They didn't carry on a conversation. No one had a clue that they even knew each other, or not as well as they did. Alex liked it. It was their little secret. The two groups hung out and played darts and pool together for hours, buying rounds of drinks. It was bar close and everyone said their goodbyes. Alex walked out of the bar and over to her car. She got a text, it was Anaconda. He texted her the snake emoji. She blushed and smiled with excitement.

She drove to Anaconda's house. He opened the door and he picked her up. He wrapped her legs around his body, and he carried her up to his room. He laid her down on the bed stripping her of her clothes. He was excited, she could see how hard he was as he slid down his pants. He put on a condom and he flipped her over. He put himself inside her and began pumping inside her forward and back, holding onto her waist thrusting into her, he then hoisted her up so he could whisper in her ear, still pumping into her, he said "I had to listen to those neanderthals talk about how hot you are all night, and it took all my restraint not to tell them you are mine, MINE!" She screamed with excitement, as he was moaning loudly, pumping into her. She gushed all over him. She had no control of her body. It was pure ecstasy every time he touched her. And it didn't matter with what. He knew how to use his mouth, tongue, hands, and cock.

Chapter 43

Mid-week Anaconda sent the snake emoji text to Alex, telling her to come over. Alex was convinced he would be disappointed when she showed up because she was on her period. She knew about the no-pants rule and was worried about bleeding through, and also worried that he would think it's gross that she was having her period. She walked into his room. He was lying in bed watching a movie. He saw her, smiled and he lifted up the blankets so she would crawl into bed. She looked at him and said. "I have my period." He said, "Ok, take off your pants and come to bed, Silly." He looked at her like he didn't care. She took off her pants. She was wearing black booty shorts and a black Eminem tank. He loved it when she came over without a bra on. He loved her breasts and he told her that often. She crawled into bed. He was wearing black boxer briefs. He spooned her and she could feel his cock rubbing up against her. He moved her hair over to one side to expose her neck and he started kissing her neck and her shoulders. He moved his hand down to her breasts, caressing them. Her flower was starting to swell, he moved his hand slowly down her stomach and to her panties. He put his hand inside her panties. She went to stop him and told him no, and reiterated that she was on her period. He said she could still come. He wanted to please her. He asked her if she had a tampon in and she said yes, he said, "Ok then." He moved his hand down to her flower and started playing with her using his fingers. She moaned. He whispered in her ear, "That's it, give it up to me." He kissed her neck. Her body jerked. She had no control. He had all the control and she had none. She moaned loudly as she came all over him. She was lost for words. She was enamored with him. She rolled over and kissed him. She looked at him with her bedroom eyes and said, "I want to love you down with my tongue." She kissed his neck, his chest, licked his tribal tattoo, and went down to his boxers and slid them off. She kissed Anaconda, licked him up and down with her tongue, and then slid him in her mouth. She stroked him as she pushed and pulled him in and out of her mouth. He started to moan, he tensed up and he shouted out as he came in her mouth. His sweet cum. It was like holy water. She loved making love to Anaconda with her mouth. She liked seeing him lose control like that.

When Alex explained her time with Anaconda to Keira, she said it was like shock waves of lightning going through her body. It almost frightened her because she had no control of it, the feeling overtook her. She once told Keira she was going to dread the day Anaconda tells her he can't be with her like that anymore. Alex's analogy was that once she and Anaconda stopped being sexual, it would be as if someone were to rip the magical horn off her unicorn.

Anaconda and Alex agreed that what they had was rare but if either of them found someone else or was interested in another person they would let the other know and let them go. They would stop sleeping with one another but would always stay close and in contact. What they had was electrifying but it was never going to be more than what it was. He was young and Alex thought he should be with someone his age, someone he could grow with, have a family with. Alex knew someday he would want that, and he deserved that without all the baggage.

Chapter 44

Alex noticed that Jess had been checking her phone a lot and said, "Jess, what's going on? Is everything ok?" Jess blushed and admitted she was getting texts from Cash. He was one of the strippers in The Lady and The Tramps. Jess and Cash were from the same small town in Iowa. She was shocked to see him up on stage last year when the girls all decided to go to one of their shows. After the show last year, Jess and Cash stayed connected. The girls all knew that Jess had a thing for Cash, but they also knew that Cash's boss had strict rules about dating while being a Tramp.

The Lady and The Tramps

The first time the girls saw The Lady and The Tramps was a year ago. Alex wasn't a huge fan of male strippers, she thought it was ridiculous to spend money just to get teased; but because the girls wanted to go, and because Alex needed to get out of the house, she decided to go with.

The show started with this strikingly, gorgeous woman out on the stage. She had long blonde hair. She looked like she was in her late 20's. She was wearing a slinky, glamorous, black sequenced gown, that hugged every curve on her body. She had tattoos all over her body, but they suited her. She was so beautiful. She looked like a piece of art. Her make-up was striking, Alex was mesmerized by her. The lady introduced herself as The Lady and she thanked the audience for being there. She announced that she had an exciting show for them and wanted to introduce her ten Tramps. One by one she named off each tramp. They came out to the stage and did a little seductive dance for the Lady. They hung on her every word, every demand, and they looked at her with adoration. After all the tramps were introduced, The Lady said in a sultry voice, "Ok gentleman, show us what you got."

Each Tramp came out one-by-one dressed up in a costume and danced a routine, as you would expect but they weren't necessarily just dancing for the audience. The act was to dance for The Lady, they were competing for her attention. The Lady would make an appearance during the acts, she would change her wardrobe, her hair, even wearing different colors and styles of wigs. The Lady and the Tramps had the audience on the edge of their seats. Alex admitted it was a unique spin to the art of strip dancing. It was one of the most entertaining and fascinating shows she had ever seen.

Jess about had a stroke when she saw Cowboy Cash strut upon the stage. She did a double-take and felt instantly flushed. Cowboy Cash was Cash from her small town. He was a few years younger than her, but she knew him to be a good, wholesome guy. He was the guy that all the local farmers would call whenever they had issues with any of their livestock. He was great with all animals. He had a natural ability to connect with them. He helped Jess's dad's heifer give birth to her first calf. The calf was breached, and Cash helped turn the calf, so the heifer could give birth to it. Jess's dad said he probably saved the life of the calf and the momma.

After the show was over, there was an opportunity to meet The Lady and the Tramps in the banquet hall. They would be there for an hour. People were allowed to meet the Tramps, take pictures with them and get autographs. Alex, being a business major was intrigued with The Lady. She wanted to know more about her background, how she came up with the idea of The Lady and The Tramps, and her business plan. The girls decided to go to the banquet hall to see if they could get up and personal with the Tramps. Jess wanted to get up and personal with one, in particular, Cash.

Jess walked right up to Cash and said hi to him. He gave her a big hug and said it was so great to see her. He said he was surprised to see her there, and she let him know that she was even more surprised to see HIM there. He chuckled and said he was using the money to pay for veterinary school. He didn't want to take out any student loans. He said it was a good gig and that the whole group was like a big family to him. Cash said it was nice seeing her, but apologized, saying he had to mingle with the crowd a little bit longer. He asked if he could call her and perhaps, they could go for coffee before they left for the next city. He had two more shows in town but was leaving Monday morning. Jess was thrilled and gave him her number.

Alex was waiting in line to talk to the Lady. A lot of the girls in front of her were asking about make-up tips and taking pictures with the beautiful temptress. She appeared to be super friendly and outgoing. Alex was next and was all business. Alex introduced herself and complimented the Lady on the show. She asked the Lady how the idea formed, how did she get it started, what was her background, where did she see it going and where did she want it to be in 10 years, and most importantly was it sustainable? The Lady looked at her and said, "Wow, inquisitive little thing, aren't you? I'd be happy to answer all your questions, but we are on a limited time crunch for the hall. We are going to be in town the rest of the weekend, leaving Monday morning. Would you like to meet up for a coffee or breakfast tomorrow morning at the little breakfast café around the corner? It would have to be early around 8:00? I make the guys start rehearsal at 10:00 AM for the evening shows." Alex told her that would be great. She was really looking forward to it.

Chapter 45

The next morning Alex met the Lady at the breakfast café. Alex learned her name was Savannah Sterling and that her story was as fascinating as she was. Her family owned a large ranch in Iowa. The ranch was passed down to her dad and uncle after her grandfather passed. Savannah had two younger brothers; they were twins. They were born when Savannah was four years old. Unfortunately, after the twins were born her mom fell into a great depression. She had a hard time taking care of the babies, she ended up leaving Savannah's dad. They haven't seen or heard from her since. Thank goodness Savannah's uncle and aunt were around to help out with the ranch and help raise Savannah and her brothers, Seth and Zach.

Savannah was the only girl, so her aunt spoiled her. Her aunt had three boys that she loved deeply but she always wanted a little girl to do girl things with. Her aunt would dress her up, put make-up on her, and would try all sorts of new hairstyles. Savannah loved how easily she could transform from a tomgirl to a beautiful princess with just the right clothes, make-up, and hair. She spent a lot of time looking at YouTube videos on how to perfect certain looks and as she got older, she had fun practicing her cosmetology skills on her aunt.

Savannah said her dad was a wreck after her mom left. He never remarried and he threw every ounce of energy into the ranch. Savannah loved that ranch. She spent as much time as possible helping her daddy. He showed her everything she needed to know about running a ranch, and he was so proud of her and happy to know that he could pass the ranch onto her.

When Savannah was just 14-years-old, her father was diagnosed with terminal cancer. He had a few surgeries and a lot of treatments, but it only prolonged the inevitable. He passed when Savannah was 17 and the boys were 13. She said the medical bills piled up. They had to sell a lot of cattle just to keep their heads above water.

Savannah dropped out of high school to help her uncle with the ranch. When she turned 18, she got her GED. She made certain her brothers continued to go to school but also gave them chores to do on the ranch before and after school. Her cousins and her brother's friends would come out to the ranch and help out too when they could. Savannah made some additional money on the side when there was a school dance or wedding. Girls would pay Savannah to do their hair and make-up. Savannah really enjoyed doing that and it made her feel good to be recognized as a make-up artist. Word gradually got around and she was offered to help do make-up and costume design for the local community theater.

Savannah's aunt was known for making the best meals for the workers at the ranch and if the weather was nice, they ate outside on the wrap-around porch that overlooked the ranch. It was so picturesque. As the years passed, Savannah's cousin's and her brother's friends became regular workers at the ranch. Savannah would always make sure there was music playing while they worked and every Friday night, she would turn on the grill, keep the drinks continuously flowing, and the music up loud. The guys, wearing their dirty jeans, muscle shirts, and sometimes no shirts, would dance along to the music, showing off their moves.

One Friday night Savannah had a couple of girls come by to get their hair and make-up done for homecoming. The girl's mothers happen to see the guys clowning around in the shed, dancing to music. Savannah saw the ladies ogle the boys. The women looked embarrassed when they realized Savannah was standing by them watching the guys dance too. Savannah nodded her head and said, "They are pretty good, aren't they? Who would have thought our small town, country boys would have moves like that?" Then one of the mothers said, "or bodies like that." The ladies laughed. Savannah told them that the guys dance around every Friday night to blow off steam so if they wanted to come by, feel free. Believe it or not, she had more customers on Friday nights over any other nights of the week. Savannah also noticed that the guys enjoyed the attention. They liked being ogled and drooled over. Savannah thought she might have something there. All these cooped-up housewives never get out or never get any young, hot action like they do on Friday nights at the Sterling Ranch. Maybe she really had something there.

Savannah talked to the director of the community theater to see if the theater had any open dates where she could book a couple of shows. The director said they had quite a few open dates. Savannah asked if she could hold three dates, one day a month for the next three months. She wanted to see if the community would be open to her idea, and if the shows were received favorably, maybe she would book more. The director nodded and told her the dates were hers.

Savannah called a Sterling Ranch Family meeting, which included everyone who worked on the ranch. She explained what she observed when the women would come over and check out the guys dance on Friday nights. She said she thought maybe they could put together some acts, incorporating the guys dancing around and maybe stripping down to whatever they felt comfortable, but never going completely nude. If they got a good turn-out, if the audience seemed to enjoy it, maybe they could book more shows, and possibly make some decent money on the side. She told them she booked three dates at the community theater for them to put on a show. One day a month for the next three months. They would advertise by flyers and word of mouth. Ticket prices were $10 a person. The guys looked shocked but excited. Then they asked her, what they would call the act, and without hesitation, she said, "We will be called The Lady and The Tramps". She thought it was fitting seeing as, they were a group of people, some family, some friends but they came together because they all needed the work. Some of the guys needed a place to stay, money, and some just liked the feeling of being a part of the Sterling Ranch Family.

The guys practiced routines every night after working all day. They were excited for the first show. The show was sold out. The 2nd and

3rd shows sold out as well. The community director asked Savannah if she was interested in booking the rest of the open dates. There was a lot of interest in the shows and the community center was making good money every time Savannah booked. Savannah ended up doubling the price of the tickets, and the women paid. All the shows were sold out. She started booking their show in other small towns, and then in bigger cities. She had ten dancers that traveled with her. Her uncle hired ranch hands to help out on the ranch when the dancers were gone. The money The Lady and The Tramps pulled in, covered all the extra expenses and then some. Now the Lady and The Tramps are well-known all over the mid-west. The ticket prices are now $45, and the shows are continuously sold out.

Savannah said it was successful because her group of guys were dedicated, and they enjoyed entertaining. Savannah told the guys to ensure the success of the business, they needed to stay single, while they were performing as Tramps. She didn't want any jealous girlfriends or wives coming and causing drama. There was also a lot of traveling and she didn't want her guys worried about a girl back home. She needed them to keep their heads in the game. If someone wanted to pursue a relationship, she was happy for them, but for the interest of the business, they could no longer be a Tramp.

It was getting close to 9:30 AM and Savannah said she needed to get back to the hotel. She enjoyed visiting with Alex and invited her to come to another show and maybe check out what they do backstage. Alex thanked Savannah for her time and for sharing her story with her. She wished her the best of luck and said she may take her up on the offer.

Chapter 46

Keira jumped in and said, "Yeah, didn't you hear that Sadie and Jess went to see The Lady and The Tramps this past weekend without us." Alex laughed and said, "Oh really? So Jess, do you have any exciting news to share with us?" Jess looked a little flushed and admitted that she has been talking a lot with Cash. They would see each other when he was in town and even if he was performing close by, she would try to meet up with him. It started out as a friendly thing; it was nice to hang out with someone from her hometown. She liked the familiarity; he knew her family and people in town. She was attracted to him and he confessed he was attracted to her too, but they couldn't date or be anything serious while he was a Tramp. Alex understood too well about forbidden love. Jess smiled and said that he wasn't going to be a Tramp anymore because he has finally saved up enough money to pay for the full four years of tuition for Veterinary School. He was accepted into the Iowa State University's Medical Veterinary School. His first day was set for January 20th. Jess was so excited. Cash told Savannah he would stay on as a Tramp until the end of December but then he was going to focus mainly on school. He will have two free weeks before his program starts. Jess said she was going to take time off and go home, visit her folks and hang out with Cash. She blushed and smiled a little girl's smile. She looked happy, really happy.

Keira looked up and her eyes lit up and she announced to the girls that eye candy just walked in the door. Alex looked up, Sadie and Jess turned around to check out the view. Jess turned beet red and she waved at the gorgeous man. It was Cash. He was wearing ripped, loose-fitting jeans, an un-tucked plaid, flannel shirt, that had most of the buttons unbuttoned. He was wearing a baseball cap, not a cowboy hat, backwards. His hair was sandy blonde, it was longer, it went past his ears but not to his shoulders. It had some curl to it. He saw Jess waving and he beamed. His teeth were pearly white. He had a nice golden tan complexion, and his dimples gave him that small town, boy charm appearance. He leisurely walked up to the table and said hi to all the ladies. He then looked directly at Jess. His eyes were a bluish-green color. Jess was still a little pink in the face, and she said "Hello." He smiled and said, "Hi". He explained he was there to drop off her necklace. He found it in his truck. It was the necklace her mom gave her before she moved to Minnesota. Jess never took it off. Jess said, "Oh wow! I didn't even notice it was gone. Thanks." Keira cleared her throat and Jess started laughing and said, "Cash, welcome to happy hour. Let me introduce you to Keira, Alex and Sadie." The girls all said hi. Cash did a polite nod and said hello again to the ladies.

Cash told Jess that they were doing some finishing touches on a couple of new routines that Savannah came up with; then they were packing up to head to the next town. He wanted to make sure he came in not only to give her the necklace but to also say bye in person. He kissed her on the cheek and said he would see her in a couple of weeks. Keira started shaking her head and waving her hand, "Wait a minute you young buck you, did you say that you were rehearsing?" He smiled, nodded, and said, "Yes, ma'am." Keira questioned, "Just at the hotel down the street right?" He nodded his head again and said, "Yes Ma'am." Keira smiled and said, "Would Ms. Savannah mind if an old lady came by to watch the rehearsal?" Keira pointed to herself, "Maybe this old lady may have some valuable feedback she would be interested in?" Cash chuckled and said, "Sure, I don't think she would mind one bit. She loves hearing people's thoughts and ideas. You might even be able to help her with a routine she has been working on. She says it's missing something, but she can't put her finger on it." He looked at Jess, Alex, and Sadie, "Do you ladies want to come?"

Keira didn't wait for anyone else to answer. She waved her hand up in the air and Jeff and Josh knew that meant she was ready for her tab. Josh arrived at the table, "Checks for everyone?" Everyone nodded their head. The girls paid up and put their coats on. Cash and Jess were walking together, Keira and Sadie were close behind and Alex was walking slowly behind the group. She wrapped her scarf around her neck loosely and she looked up at Jeff and Josh to wave goodbye. As she waved, she saw Josh was talking to a customer up at the bar. Josh waved back and the customer turned to see who Josh was waving to. The customer and Alex locked eyes. It was Dr. Heart.

Alex hadn't seen Dr. Heart for over a year, almost two. There were a couple of times she saw him in the hall at the hospital and they would quickly glance at each other and wave hi, but that was it. She hadn't seen him out, and especially not at Oscar's. She thought maybe he was avoiding it because he knew she went there so frequently or maybe it was by chance that they just didn't drink at the same places at the same time in over a year. She noticed he was there by himself, bellied up at the bar. His hair was now short and spiked on top. He was strikingly handsome. He and Alex smiled at each other. His steel-blue eyes gleamed from across the room. She saw his dimples. She felt flushed, nervous, her heart ached and raced with excitement, and her stomach filled with butterflies.

Cash was holding the door open for the ladies. Keira turned around to make sure Alex was coming. She saw Alex waving at Josh, she also saw who Josh was talking to. She looked at Alex's face. She recognized that smile, but she also recognized the pain in her face. Alex quickly looked over at Keira and smiled. She grabbed Keira's hand and said "Hey Sex Kitten, why don't you go on without me. You know the whole stripping thing isn't my thing." Keira nodded her head and hugged Alex tightly and spoke softly to her, "Ok, sweet girl. You know he was right; your heart can love more than one person." Keira kissed Alex on the cheek and said, "I love you... and don't worry, I will fill you in on everything that happens tonight." She let out a mischievous giggle and then hooped and hollered as she pranced out the door.

Alex looked at the doctor and slowly walked up to him. She asked him if the stool next to him was taken and he smiled and shook his head no and offered her to sit. Josh poured a Captain Diet and decorated it with enough limes to make it look like a palm tree. He winked at Alex as she sat down next to Dr. Heart.

The End.

CPSIA information can be obtained
at www.ICGtesting.com
Printed in the USA
JSHW050825250222
23323JS00004B/13